"You had no right to read your mother's diary, Maggie,"

Kyle told Mary's daughter. "Much less show it to me."

"You don't think so?" Maggie asked. She appeared to be truly surprised.

"Of course," Kyle said. "Privacy is something a person—"

"I mean," Maggie interrupted, "I thought since you two had, you know...that you might find it interesting."

Kyle decided to try another angle. "I know it must seem odd to you that your mother and I...you know." He wasn't able to articulate the bare truth any better than Maggie had.

But Maggie waved his words away. "Oh, I don't care about that," she said, turning to face him. She watched him for a moment, but Kyle was clueless as to how she expected him to respond.

"Jeez, you adults are so dense sometimes," Maggie said finally. She narrowed her penetrating stare. "Hasn't it occurred to you that you're my father?"

Dear Reader,

Happy Valentine's Day! Love is in the air...and between every page of a Silhouette Romance novel. Treat yourself to six new stories guaranteed to remind you what Valentine's Day is all about....

In Liz Ireland's *The Birds and the Bees,* Kyle Weston could truly be a FABULOUS FATHER. That's why young Maggie Moore would do *anything* to reunite him with his past secret love—her mother, Mary.

You'll find romance and adventure in Joleen Daniels's latest book, *Jilted!* Kidnapped at the altar, Jenny Landon is forced to choose between the man she truly loves— and the man she *must* marry.

The legacy of SMYTHESHIRE, MASSACHUSETTS continues in Elizabeth August's *The Seeker.*

Don't miss the battle of wills when a fast-talking lawyer tries to woo a sweet-tongued rancher back to civilization in Stella Bagwell's *Corporate Cowgirl.* Jodi O'Donnell takes us back to the small-town setting of her first novel in *The Farmer Takes a Wife.* And you'll be SPELLBOUND by Pat Montana's handsome— and magical—hero in this talented author's first novel, *One Unbelievable Man.*

Happy reading!

Anne Canadeo
Senior Editor

Please address questions and book requests to:
Reader Service
U.S.: P.O. Box 1325, Buffalo, NY 14269
Canadian: P.O. Box 1050, Niagara Falls, Ont. L2E 7G7

THE BIRDS AND THE BEES

Liz Ireland

Silhouette
ROMANCE™

Published by Silhouette Books

America's Publisher of Contemporary Romance

For Julianne, the coolest person I know

 SILHOUETTE BOOKS

ISBN 0-373-08988-0

THE BIRDS AND THE BEES

Books by Liz Ireland

Silhouette Romance

Man Trap #963
The Birds and the Bees #988

LIZ IRELAND

worked at jobs that ranged from actress to book editor before deciding to concentrate on writing. A former resident of Brooklyn, New York, she now lives in her native state of Texas with her two cats, Henry and Agnes.

Fabulous Fathers

Kyle Weston on Fatherhood...

Dear Maggie,

It's too late for Dr. Spock. I've missed your first word, your first steps and your first day of school. Now you're asking me to leap into fatherhood at the most difficult point—just in time to share all your teen troubles. And knowing you, you'll have plenty of those. And knowing me, I'll make plenty of blunders.

I wish I could be the dad of your dreams, James Dean in the flesh. But most of all, Maggie, I want to give you the family you've never had, the one I deprived you of by running away before you were born. When I didn't know you existed.

From here on out, I swear I'll be the hippest, coolest dad on the planet. That is, if we can just get your wonderful, stubborn mom to cooperate....

Love,
Kyle

Prologue

The giant purple bubble grew and expanded and shone in the late afternoon sun. It exploded suddenly, but Maggie Moore sucked in her breath at precisely the right second, and the brilliant creation once again became a grape-flavored wad of gum in her mouth. None had stuck to her nose or lips. Maggie cracked the gum against her molars in satisfaction.

"That was a good one," her friend Winona said.

Maggie rolled her eyes. Really, Winona was very uncool. As many times as Maggie had tried explaining it to her, she couldn't grasp the concept that mature almost-thirteen-year-olds weren't supposed to be impressed by certain things anymore. And bubble gum was one of them.

Ignoring the comment, she reached again for the spiral notebook that had been the focus of so much of her attention lately. It was in fairly good shape, considering that it was older than Maggie herself. Still, she was always careful when sneaking a peek at the book. Especially today, since this was the first time she had taken it out of the house.

But she was feeling bolder now, and more desperate. After discovering her mother's diary—tightly guarded in the rolltop desk in Mary Moore's bedroom—Maggie had felt restless, just as she always did when guarding something secret that she didn't quite understand. She had finally convinced Winona to skip ballet class with her and take a look at the diary and its incredible disclosures.

"K.W.," she mused. "Those initials are the key to everything."

"I don't know, Maggie," Winona said. "I just can't see your mother...you know."

"Having an affair."

Both girls winced to hear the words spoken aloud, although Winona was more visible in her revulsion. Even though they had seen all the films in health class, especially an informative, titillating one called *Beyond the Birds and the Bees,* and Winona's parents had given her an old-fashioned talking-to about the facts of life, the two friends agreed that the physical side of things sounded a little unappealing. And in relation to Maggie's four-square mother, words like "sex" and "affairs" seemed almost incomprehensible. But there it was, in clear black-and-white perfect handwriting, right in her mother's spiral notebook...

"It really wasn't an affair, though," Maggie corrected. "According to the diary, she did *it* with K.W. before she even considered marrying my dad."

"You said the diary barely even mentions your dad."

"Yeah." Maggie thought for a moment. "It ends right at Christmas, when K.W. dumped her."

"Your poor mom," Winona said with a melodramatic sigh.

"And then I was born at the end of the next September."

Winona counted on her fingers. "Phew."

"Man, that just about explains everything." Maggie reached into her knapsack and pulled out a crumpled pack of cigarettes.

"Maggie..." Winona's voice wavered.

"Don't be dumb. Nobody's gonna see us." Nevertheless, she looked furtively toward Mrs. Williamson's backyard. The old lady barely said two words in a day, but when she did, it was usually to complain about Maggie. But the only living being in view was Fritz, Mrs. Williamson's black French poodle.

"What if your mother comes home early?"

"My mother?" Maggie cupped her hands as she lighted a match and took that first nauseating puff of tobacco. "My mother hasn't left work early in all the years she's worked at that place."

"Still..."

Maggie waved away her friend's protests. She was much more interested in fathers than mothers at the moment. Just contemplating the possibility that she wasn't spawned from two lifelong pencil pushers gave her hope for the future. "K.W. I bet *he* wasn't an accountant," Maggie said. "And I bet that's why I'm not like my mom."

"You look exactly like your mom."

Maggie's expression turned frigid. Winona could really get on her nerves sometimes. "But there's just something different about me. James Dean and I have more in common than my mom and I do."

"You still look just like Mrs. Moore," Winona insisted.

"Yeah, but my mom's a *secretary*. And my *supposed* father was an accountant. Do I strike you as a cross between a secretary and an accountant?"

Winona looked anxiously at her friend. Maggie was wearing her favorite denim jacket, the one with zippers all over it, which was the closest thing to a leather jacket that Mrs. Moore would allow her daughter to wear. Her curly brown hair still had orange highlights from when they tried to dye it red last fall. To Winona, Maggie was the embodiment of cool, and the crowning emblem of her taste, even better than the jacket with zippers, was her blue jeans. Together, they had shot them full of holes with Maggie's grandfather's hunting rifle. Without permission.

Maggie was nervy, cool and the best friend Winona had ever had. She was definitely not secretary material. And anyway, Winona feared Maggie would belt her if she said that she was. "Nope," Winona said finally. "I guess you're right about having a different dad."

"Man!" Maggie hooted triumphantly, as if Winona's opinion made her hunch as official as a birth certificate. "I knew it! What do you think K.W. stands for? It's just like Mother to have written her diary in code."

"Hmm." Winona thought for a moment. "What about Kevin?"

Maggie wrinkled her nose. "Not!"

"Like Kevin Costner."

That gave Maggie pause. Maybe a Kevin for a father wouldn't be so bad, after all. Still... "Kevin Costner's nothing like James Dean. I bet my dad looked just like James Dean, don't you? I bet he wore a leather bomber jacket, just like the one I want."

"Maybe that's why you want it in the first place. Maybe you're still connected somehow to your real dad. You know, like psychically or something."

Maggie raised her eyebrows. Coming from Winona, that was pretty heavy stuff. Maybe her friend wasn't hopeless after all. Thinking, she dug a hole in the Bermuda grass and snubbed out her cigarette in the dirt. "I just wish my mother would've been more detailed. Can you imagine being in love with someone, *sleeping* with someone, and not even saying what they looked like in your diary?"

Winona shook her head. "Are you sure she didn't?"

"I've read that thing twenty times." Maggie let out a frustrated huff. "All she ever wrote about were her *feelings*. I mean, what's the point in keeping a diary if you aren't going to put down the cold, hard facts?"

Her friend shrugged in sympathy. "I guess you're going to have to be extracreative if you're going to find out who your real dad is."

"Easier said than done," Maggie said skeptically. "What bright ideas can you come up with?"

"Well..." A look of pure, on-the-spot panic crossed Winona's face. She gulped, then piped up hesitantly, "Like, you said your mom still works at that same advertising company, right?"

"Yeah?" Maggie crossed her arms.

"Well, like, if K.W. worked there, too, maybe he still does."

The words hit Maggie with the force of a blow. "You're right!"

"You should go to your mom's office and see if you can find a phone list or something, and see if there's a guy with the initials K.W. working there."

Maggie felt humbled. Why hadn't she thought of this? She couldn't believe that Winona, of all people, had come up with such a sensible, helpful tip. But of course, Winona didn't have such a stake in the outcome. She knew for a fact that her father was just a grocer.

"I'm gonna catch a bus over there right now," Maggie said, carefully stuffing the diary into her backpack.

"Holy cow!" Winona cried, looking at her watch.

Maggie cringed. Just when she thought her friend was showing promise, Winona started sounding like a dork again. "Don't worry, you'll be back at the ballet school in time for your mother to pick you up. Just don't be so jumpy. You look guilty."

"My mom would just kill me if she knew I skipped."

Maggie popped a fresh piece of purple gum into her mouth. "She won't. You give these grown-ups too much credit."

They left Maggie's backyard through the side gate and began to hike toward the bus stop. Winona chattered on about the various ways her mother would punish her if she were ever to find out she'd cut ballet class, which made Maggie wonder why Winona bothered to skip at all. Maggie didn't care herself. If her mother asked her, she'd give her usual excuse—after-school activities were for morons.

No, she had more important things on her mind, like hunting down an acceptably cool father figure. She just had to find him. How was she supposed to grow up sane while living with a secretary, when anyone could tell she had the soul of a James Dean?

At least now she had one lead, although the chances that this K.W. person would still be working at her mom's company seemed pretty slim.

Chapter One

"Kyle Weston, please," demanded the silky, sultry voice on the other end of the phone. The voice of Cindy Sellars.

Mary Moore tried to keep herself from bristling. Who Kyle Weston spent his quality time with was no concern of hers. Of course, given the fact that this woman had opted for cheerleading as a lifetime profession, Mary wondered just how high the quality of time with her could be.

"Just a moment," Mary said, "I'll see if he's still here." He was, and she knew it, but it gave her a wicked kind of pleasure to hear Cindy's helpless sputtering right before she hit the Hold button.

Honestly, she was beginning to think Maggie was wearing off on her. Putting people on hold just to annoy them sounded like something her twelve-year-old daughter would really relate to—as far as she would admit to relating to anything as mundane as clerical work, Mary mentally corrected.

Which reminded her, it was nearly five o'clock, and she had to pick Maggie up from ballet. Mary scurried around her cubicle, making sure the hatches were battened down for the night. In work as in her private life, she was very particular about keeping things in their rightful place and properly guarded.

Now if I can just do that with my emotions, too, everything will be okay.

But she was beginning to doubt whether she possessed that kind of fortitude. Each day she was forced to sit outside Kyle Weston's office, screening his calls and typing his memos, was agony. And she'd been his secretary for a month already! Wasn't this supposed to get easier?

"Good night, Mrs. Moore," boomed the voice of Arlen Zieglar, president of Zieglar and Weston Advertising.

"Good night, Mr. Zieglar," Mary answered, but Zieglar was already in the elevator. The elderly man, who had been plagued by sinus problems and creative block for more than a decade, was now more a company figurehead than anything else. But he prided himself on knowing every employee's name.

If only she was *his* secretary, Mary thought yearningly. What a cushy job that would be. Arlen Zieglar hadn't personally handled a major account since the Tasty Morsel TV Dinner campaign in the seventies. He didn't even travel anymore. And he surely didn't date.

Her boss, on the other hand, was the company dynamo—and apparently still going strong in the hormone department. After thirteen years in California building his own rival ad agency, Kyle Weston had come back to Dallas a little over a month ago to take the reigns from his father. Kyle, Sr. died not long after, and the son inherited his father's office, client list and secretary—much to Mary's displeasure.

For a few weeks there, she thought she could handle it. After all, it had been years since she had even thought about Kyle, at least as anyone other than the boss's son. But now he was the boss, *her* boss, which seemed to intimately link them somehow. She was in charge of his correspondence, his company accounts and his appointment calendar. She had to hash out his travel arrangements and make his dinner reservations. Tonight, for instance, she knew that he had a table reserved at a pricey French restaurant on Turtle Creek . . . a table for two.

Mary gasped and looked at the phone panel. The Hold button winked angrily at her. She hadn't meant to torment Cindy for so long.

She punched in Kyle's extension and picked up the receiver. "I'm putting you through now," she said cheerily.

"For heaven's sake—" squawked the disembodied voice.

Mary pressed Transfer before she could hear any more. Good grief, was she losing her mind? She had always prided herself on her professional courtesy, but after a month of being Kyle Weston's personal secretary, she was now resorting to petty phone shenanigans.

The telephone rang again as Mary was shrugging on her jacket. She picked up the receiver, praying it wasn't a lengthy business matter—or Cindy Sellars calling back to chew her out.

"Hello?" she said into the phone.

"Allo, Mrs. Moore? This is Madame Jarde!"

As though she could have mistaken her for someone else, Mary thought, her shoulders sagging. That thickly accented, authoritarian voice could only mean one thing.

"*Encore,* your Maggie has skipped *le ballet!*"

"Oh, Madame Jarde, I'm so very, very sorry," Mary apologized. "I had no idea." Just speaking to the woman made *her* feel like she was twelve years old again.

"This is a fine mess, *non?* What are we going to do with a girl who will not come to class, will not practice and refuses to take off her sneakers for *le ballet,* uh?"

"Yes, well, I've told her—"

"We have a recital coming up, Mrs. Moore. A girl who cannot dance at a recital is *une probleme.*"

"I can try—"

"*Bien.* But you should know that Maggie is not progressing as she should be!"

Click. Mary stared at the receiver in her hand for several moments. That French woman scared the wits out of her sometimes. As she reached to return the phone to its cradle, she knocked over her mug of tea, which spilled across her desk and down her khaki-colored skirt. Mary jumped back and unlocked her top desk drawer to get a napkin.

What did her daughter have against dancing, she wondered as she swiped a paper towel across herself and her desk top. It was supposed to have been a fun after-school activity, but Maggie made her feel like an ogress for spending good money to send her there. Mary didn't know what else to do. Children—everyone, in her opinion—needed structure, routine. If Maggie had her way, she would spend her life in front of the television, watching James Dean movies on videocassette.

Her behavior was completely out of Mary's realm of experience. When she was a teenager, she had never been rebellious. And she had never had such bizarre notions as Maggie came up with—like blowing her blue jeans to kingdom come with a rifle. Where did she come up with these ideas? And James Dean? The man had been dead for thirty years!

"Mrs. Moore, can I speak to you for a moment?"

The deep voice snapped Mary out of her thoughts and into a brand-new crisis. "Yes, Mr. Weston," she said, ditching the sticky, drenched paper towel in the wastebasket.

She followed her boss into his generous office, wincing slightly at the unpleasant dampness of her skirt chafing against her knee. If only Kyle hadn't needed to talk to her, she could have dried off more thoroughly. And if Maggie hadn't skipped ballet, she wouldn't have spilled the tea in the first place. But of course, if Cindy Sellars hadn't called, she would have taken the mug to the kitchen...

"Are you okay?"

Kyle Weston's brown eyes locked on hers, as if he could gauge her emotional state by staring hard enough. As usual, his gaze only threw her more off balance. Then, when his eyes traveled down to her tea-stained front, she felt even shakier still. Why, she asked herself for the umpteenth time, why couldn't he have stayed in California?

"I'm fine," she lied, just wanting to get this last encounter of the day over with. In deference to her drippy skirt, she remained standing, her pen poised over a legal pad she held in the crook of her arm.

Kyle looked at her strangely as he sat down behind his huge oak desk. Even seated, his muscular six-foot frame was imposing. Mary kept her eyes on the pad and was grateful when he cleared his throat to begin.

"Just a few things..." His voice trailed off, and Mary looked up and saw Kyle's concerned expression. "Are you going to do this standing up?" he asked.

Mary blinked innocently. "I had thought so, Mr. Weston, but if you'd rather I was sitting—"

"No, please, I was just curious." He cleared his throat again, then stood up himself and began pacing behind the desk. "Just a few things," he said. "I won't be here tomorrow, so if the Canine Gourmet people call, transfer them to Ben Sykes in graphics."

"All right," Mary replied, making a quick note. Kyle had stopped his pacing, and she glanced up. He was looking at her with an odd, almost curious expression. "Is there anything else?"

"Uh..." Kyle hesitated. "I had some dinner reservations that I need to cancel, but—"

"La Maison at eight o'clock? I'll cancel them on my way out."

"If you're sure it's no trouble," Kyle said.

"It's my job," Mary reminded him. She tried to remain professional, although her mind was abuzz with speculation. Had his date bowed out?

"The lady has...other plans for our evening together." Kyle smiled, almost enjoying watching Mary cover her embarrassment. God, this was horrible. Why, he asked for the thousandth time, why couldn't Mary have been assigned to Arlen Zieglar instead of his father?

For weeks now they had been tap-dancing around each other, trying to pretend that they were business-on-the-brain automatons. It was a relief to finally bring up his personal life around Mary—although a date with Cindy was hardly tantamount to a fulfilling social occasion. But it at least broached a subject for them to take up rather than memos and meetings.

But apparently, Mary had no plans to assuage her curiosity. "Is that all, Mr. Weston?" she asked, obviously impatient to make her escape.

Kyle was giving her that look again, that intense stare that made her want to flee from the room. Mary turned back to her legal pad. This was what came of youthful indiscretion, she thought. Not only had she suffered the humiliation of rejection and valiantly soldiered her way through the consequences of her folly, but now, a full thirteen years later, she found herself trapped in an agonizing limbo of discomfort. Surely this was more punishment, but how much sadder and wiser could she get?

"That's definitely not all," Kyle said, letting out a frustrated breath. "I want to know what's wrong, and you can drop the Mr. Weston."

Mary's head snapped up. Kyle could practically hear her gulp. "Wrong?" she asked.

"Mary," he said, using her name for the first time in years, "you look completely preoccupied. And wet. Is something the matter?"

Mary searched her brain for an appropriate response. She said the first thing that popped into her mind. "I'm late picking up my daughter." She didn't add that she didn't know precisely where her daughter was.

"I'm sorry," Kyle said, glancing at his watch. Damn. Apparently this wasn't a good time to hash out some way to reach a better working relationship between them. "Never mind the reservations—"

"Oh, no—I wasn't complaining."

"That's just it," Kyle put in. "Complain, I don't mind. Your daughter is more important than my dinner."

Mary took a step back. His tone had an unfamiliar, personal edge to it that made her uncomfortable. And he was standing so close, trapping her between the chair and the ficus tree in the corner. Worse, it was impossible to see him, to be so close to those broad shoulders and strong arms, and not remember. Heat flooded her face.

He had changed very little over the years. His dark blond hair was cut shorter and the edges of his eyes and mouth were creased a little, but at thirty-five Kyle Weston still had a jaunty youthfulness about him. And he still had a way of looking at her that made her insides melt.

He reached over and put a hand on her shoulder. "Maggie, isn't it?"

Mary swallowed. The heat and pressure of his hand, even through the fabric of her jacket and blouse, unnerved her. "Maggie?" she asked.

"Your daughter."

"Oh." Good grief, she was mooning over her boss! She shook her head, then took another step backward, grasping for control of the situation. "Yes," she said, "and I really must pick her up from ballet class. She's been taking lessons for two years now. She's quite talented."

If nothing else, Mary thought, she didn't want Kyle to think of her as a haphazard mother, although lately she was feeling that way herself. As infuriating as she could be, Maggie was still someone she was proud of.

"How old is she?" Kyle asked.

"Twelve."

"Does she give you trouble?" he asked, chuckling. "I know I was a regular hellion at that age."

"Well, Maggie's father was a responsible person," Mary blurted out, then just stopped herself from clapping her hand over her stupid mouth. The words had come out more sharply than she had meant them to. What was the matter with her? She supposed she wasn't comfortable talking about Maggie—and her late husband—with Kyle.

"I really should be going," she said quickly. "I'll take care of those reservations on the way out."

"Don't bother," Kyle said apologetically.

"It's no trouble."

Kyle followed her to the door. Impulsively, as they reached the outside of his office, he touched her elbow. "You're a wonder, Mary."

Her breath caught as their eyes met. She was a wonder, he realized. For weeks—hell, for years—guilt over the way he had treated her had nagged at his conscience, blotting out the memory of how it had been between them. Now, looking into her clear blue eyes, he remembered.

He still found her girl-next-door prettiness completely magnetic. Her skin seemed irresistibly creamy and smooth, and suddenly he felt and just barely stifled the urge to gently rub his palm across her cheek. And her lips, lips that seemed too rarely to turn up in a smile, seemed to beckon him now. Or maybe he just imagined...

"Oh, man!"

At the sound of Maggie's voice, Mary froze. Kyle's eyes, so smoky and seductive just a split second before, revealed pure bewilderment. Mary felt the same confusion. Given another moment, she would have gone beyond simply mooning over her boss—she had practically been ready to pounce on him!

Saved by the daughter. But what was Maggie doing here?

Mary ducked out of Kyle's hold and turned, but the question on her lips died when she saw Maggie. Her daughter was staring, not at her or Kyle, but at the rectangular brass nameplate on the door behind them. Her mouth gaping, she appeared oblivious to the two very curious adults watching her.

"Maggie?" Mary prompted.

"Huh?" With obvious effort, Maggie tore her gaze from the nameplate and gave Mary a disapproving once-over. "Gosh, Mom, what happened? It looks like your lap got caught in a flood."

Mary felt her face go beet red and tried in vain to retain some dignity. She had forgotten about the skirt. Kyle must have thought she was an idiot. "I just spilled some tea," she explained.

"I guess this is your daughter," Kyle said, extending his hand toward Maggie. "I'm Kyle Weston."

"You're Kyle Weston?" Maggie shook his hand limply, her sharp gaze alternating between the man and his nameplate. "You mean, you're my mom's... boss?"

Kyle laughed. "This is the nineties. We prefer 'officiating co-worker' or 'managing superior.'"

Maggie pulled her hand back, managing a lame, half-embarrassed laugh. She crossed one leg over the other and dug her hands deep inside her denim jacket, but Mary noticed that instead of staring at the floor in her usual manner, Maggie kept her eyes trained on Kyle.

"Well," Mary chirped, "I guess we should be on our way."

"How was ballet?" Kyle asked.

"Ballet?" Maggie echoed, obviously alarmed. She glanced nervously at Mary, then back to Kyle. "Class was canceled."

Mary felt her mouth pucker into a displeased maternal purse. "Maggie..." she said in warning.

Maggie rose to the challenge. "There was a note on the door saying that the teacher's father was in the hospital and she couldn't make it," she elaborated, "so I came here, to save you the drive to the school."

"That was big of you." Mary grimaced. However much she wanted to scold, she was stuck. There was no way she was going to let Kyle in on the fact that her daughter was lying—especially when she'd just been bragging about her.

As if reading her thoughts, Kyle said, "Your mom tells me you're quite a dancer."

"*Me?*" Maggie asked incredulously, turning to her mother for confirmation.

"We really should be going."

"If you ever have a recital, I'd be happy to come."

Both Maggie and Mary whirled on him, stunned. "You would?" Mary asked, suspicious.

"Sure," Kyle said breezily.

"You must not have much of a life," Maggie blurted out.

"Maggie!"

"Heck," Maggie said in her own defense, "I can think of a million better things to do than go to a gross recital."

Kyle had to fight to keep from roaring with laughter. Now, this was a kid he could relate to. Gauging by her expression, though, Mary was not quite so amused by her daughter's forthrightness.

"We really should be going," she repeated.

"Why?" Maggie asked, again staring at Kyle. She seemed to take in his gray suit with more than her usual distaste.

Honestly, Mary thought, she was going to have to remind her daughter of her manners again—and till doomsday, if Maggie's behavior to date was any indication. She took a deep breath. "Well, for one thing, tonight is the night we have dinner with Mrs. Williamson."

Maggie had the good grace not to moan, even though Mary knew she viewed their weekly trip to the Brass Kettle with their elderly neighbor as nothing short of torture. Instead, she shuffled her feet and, amazingly, held out a hand to Kyle. "It was nice meeting you, Mr. Weston."

Kyle grasped the hand. "Sure thing, Maggie," he said, then reached over and patted the girl on the shoulder. "Keep up the good work. According to your mom, you're a model kid."

"Grounded, for a month. Is that understood?"

Maggie nodded, looking absently out at the passing street. "What does Mr. Weston do?"

"I told you, he's the head of Zieglar and Weston," Mary said, braking for a light. "But don't try to change the subject. Why did you skip ballet today?"

Maggie shrugged. "I dunno." She couldn't work up much zeal for their usual mother-daughter battle. She was too disappointed.

Kyle Weston was a dud. She should have suspected he would be when Winona's clue led right to him. Nothing good came that easily. And sure enough, K.W., the elusive father of her dreams, had turned out to be just another pencil pusher in a suit. Maggie fought back the urge to cry; the unfairness of it all seemed overwhelming.

"Maggie, are you listening to me?"

"Huh?"

"Oh, Maggie," Mary moaned, still maneuvering carefully through traffic, "what am I going to do with you?"

In spite of her anguish, Maggie felt a smile tug at her lips. "I don't know, but if I'm gonna be grounded for a month, you'd better think of something fast."

Mary laughed, then stopped herself. She had to show Maggie she was serious. "I was saying, I talked to Madame Jarde today."

"What else does Mr. Weston do?" Maggie asked out of the blue.

"What?"

"Like, what does he do for fun?"

Mary thought for a moment. Why was Maggie so interested in her boss? "I don't know, Maggie," she answered with a sigh. "I just know him from work."

Maggie knew that was a lie. Unless . . . but no, Kyle Weston had to be K.W. She could tell just by the lovey-dovey way he and her mom were staring at each other when she found them. She shivered at the memory. Gushiness from two people as old as they were just didn't seem natural.

"I don't even think he's that good-looking," she said aloud.

"Who?"

Maggie rolled her eyes. "C'mon, Mother. Kyle Weston."

"You don't? I mean—" Flustered, Mary cut her eyes in Maggie's direction. "Well, for heaven's sake, why should he be? Besides, you can't judge a book by its cover, you know."

Yup, Kyle Weston was definitely the one. Her mother could be goofy, but only when she was really muddled did she start talking in kindergarten-teacher phrases. "He doesn't look anything like James Dean," Maggie said.

"Oh, Maggie," Mary said, half laughing. She stopped herself again. Firm, she had to be firm. "Which reminds me, there will be no James Dean movies while you're grounded."

"What!"

"You need to pay more attention to your real commitments and less to oily movie stars."

"That's not fair!" Maggie protested. "My life is nothing but commitments to all these little piddly activities. Those movies are the only fun I have."

Her words tore at Mary. Were they true? Sometimes she hated being a mother—hated herself for having to sound like one. "Those 'piddly activities' were supposed to be fun," she explained. "And if nothing else, they're to teach responsibility. Like showing up."

Maggie crossed her arms and slumped in her seat. "It's still not fair," she grumbled.

Nothing was fair. A month without James Dean? How was she going to survive? Especially now, when she needed him more than ever. He would know just how it was to discover—twice in one lifetime!—that your father was a working stiff.

Kyle gunned the engine of his snappy red sports car and peeled out of the Zieglar and Weston parking lot. Okay, it was a childish gesture, but this had been an insane day. Had he really been about to kiss his secretary in front of the entire office? Never had he even contemplated doing something so unprofessional. At least, not in almost fifteen years—since the last time he'd worked with Mary. And then he'd done much more than contemplate.

Burning rubber in the empty parking lot did little to ease his frustration. Maybe his date with Cindy would calm him down, but he doubted it. He was tired, and Cindy had called that afternoon to say that she wanted to go dancing, not to some stuffy restaurant. The thought of dancing the night away made Kyle squirm. Wasn't he too old for things like that?

Mary probably would have opted for the restaurant.

Kyle shook his head. He just couldn't stop thinking about her. And it wasn't just because she was beautiful, although he'd always been attracted to her. No, it was more than that. She had something more. She had . . . maturity.

The irony of that last thought almost made him laugh out loud. Thirteen years ago, he had fled Dallas, fled Mary, because of her maturity. As a college-graduate intern at his dad's company, he'd pursued her for months. And she'd put him off, until the office Christmas party, when they'd both had too much champagne and one thing led to another. After their one-night stand, Mary had known what she wanted. Marriage. To him.

Nothing would have made his father happier than to see him settled down in Dallas, working for the family business, with a wife and maybe even some kids. But pleasing his father was about the last thing Kyle had been interested in when he was twenty-two. For his whole life, Kyle, Sr. had dictated what schools he would go to, what people he should mingle with, what activities he should involve himself in. Kyle had taken the internship at Zieglar and Weston as a last concession. But that morning, when Mary started talking marriage, he'd freaked. One week later, he'd boarded a plane for Los Angeles.

Since then, his life had been one long holiday from responsibility. Oh, he'd started his own agency and built a reputation in business, but in his personal life, he had pursued the L.A. bachelor's dream—great house, fast cars, beautiful women. And no commitments.

Frankly, it was a hell of a way to spend a decade. Until one day when he looked around and saw that his friends were all married and living in the suburbs. Attendance at his renowned parties dropped dramatically as his cohorts became more interested in Little League than whooping it up. They'd traded in their fast cars for mini vans, and seemed happier for it.

And then, about three months ago, his father had called from the hospital. Kyle came down to help out while he recuperated, but after a while it became obvious to them both that Kyle, Sr. wasn't getting any better. After the funeral it just seemed natural to stay on in his father's house and take over his father's half of the business.

So here he was, in Dallas, living the very life he had fled. And the biggest kicker of all was that Mary's domestic little dreams, once anathema to him, looked pretty good now from where he was standing.

Maybe because her life was so much richer than his. He'd heard about her quick marriage after he'd moved to Los Angeles, and how her husband had died in a car accident not long after. But look what she'd made of her life. She'd slaved away for nearly fifteen years to become an executive secretary, while he'd practically had his professional life handed to him. She'd had a marriage, albeit a short one, and now she had a daughter.

The memory of Maggie in his office that afternoon made him laugh. In spite of Mary's presenting her as the proverbial little angel, Kyle suspected that kid could be a heap of trouble. To Mary's credit, she didn't seem to try to stifle her daughter's straightforward manner the way some parents would. Like his father had. From his own experience, he knew that strict control often gave way to a complete loss of control.

As he pulled into his driveway, he was annoyed to see his neighbor, Sam Terry, clipping the hedge that bordered their properties. Sam, the eyes and ears of the neighborhood, practically lay in wait for his neighbors as they came home, usually under the guise of doing yard work. More than anything else, Sam loved to hear about the lives of unmarried people.

"Hey," Sam called as Kyle got out of his car. Kyle took off his sunglasses and waited as Sam approached him with his hedge clippers. "Comin' home early, aren't ya', bud?"

"Yeah, well, I really don't have much time to talk, Sam. I'm going right back out as soon as I can jump in and out of the shower."

"Date?"

"Yeah. I'll see you—"

"I tell ya'," Sam drawled, waylaying Kyle's exit. "You bachelors have it made. You takin' her out on your bike?" Sam loved to hear the details.

"I guess so." In fact, Kyle knew so. Cindy had pointedly stressed that she'd just bought a new leather outfit that would go perfectly with his motorcycle.

"A girl and a bike." Sam sighed wistfully. "Me and the ball and chain are probably gonna be eating Lean Cuisine and watching *I Dream of Jeannie* reruns again. You going out to eat?"

"Dancing."

"Yeah, boy. You've got a life, all right."

Kyle wished he could get so wound up about it himself. He would even welcome a TV dinner at this point. Cindy rarely ate anything. Even though she was no longer a professional cheerleader, she said she still had to diet. Old habits died hard, Kyle supposed.

But dancing? Somehow, he couldn't imagine Cindy two-stepping or ballroom dancing. He certainly hoped she wasn't going to drag him to one of those freaky nightclub places she was always yammering on about. He was getting a little long in the tooth for slam dancing…or whatever people did these days.

"Say, did you hear it was going to rain tonight?"

"No," Kyle said. Good, he could call Cindy and tell her they were going to take the car. Maybe he could even convince her to punt the dancing and go straight to her Jacuzzi instead. They could get take-out Chinese.

"Yeah," Sam droned on, "they've been forecasting rain all day. Guess that wouldn't stop a swinger like you, though."

"Right, Sam," Kyle said, slapping his neighbor genially on the shoulder. "You have a nice evening with the wife."

Sam beamed. "Yeah, you're the lucky one, all right. I envy you, bud."

Once inside his house, Kyle headed straight for the shower, shucking his clothes on his way to the bathroom. As he stepped under the water, his stomach growled angrily. In spite of Sam's adulation of his bachelor status, Kyle could build up little enthusiasm for the coming evening. If it weren't for the Jacuzzi at the end of the tunnel, he might have called Cindy to cancel. And frankly, at this point he didn't care if Cindy was in that Jacuzzi with him or not; he just wanted to relax. He'd probably want to even more after a night of dancing.

Kyle dropped his head back and let the water sluice over him. Sam was crazy. He had a gorgeous wife and two cute kids. Kyle sometimes watched the Terry children playing in their immaculately trimmed backyard. Then he would look over to his own empty yard, the same one he had played in when he was little, which now held nothing except a rusting exercise bike and a covered swimming pool. In his weaker moments, he sometimes tried to envision how a swing set and a jungle gym would look back there.

His father had warned him. Especially during those last weeks, Kyle, Sr. had grilled Kyle about when he was going to settle down and have kids. He'd regret it if he didn't, the older man had warned.

Kyle had just laughed. His mother and father had never seemed like the perfect couple, and his less-than-idyllic relationship with his father had always discouraged Kyle from even thinking about a family of his own. Now his father was gone, and all Kyle had of his family was this cavernous house and his job. Suddenly, it seemed that the only things he really wanted were precisely what he'd spent his entire life scoffing at. Stability, family...love.

Think of the Jacuzzi, he reminded himself. He was still skeptical about love and all that stuff, anyway. Besides, good solid families were hard to come by these days. Kyle laughed. Life would be a cinch if a man could just pick up a family ready-made.

Chapter Two

"Sure is raining hard," Mrs. Williamson said.

Maggie let out an elongated, tortured sigh.

"Yes, it is," Mary replied. She had the sinking feeling that she had just experienced the bulk of the conversation for the evening.

As they sat at their usual table at the Brass Kettle, waiting for their meal, the three of them fidgeted and coughed sporadically. Mrs. Williamson was being especially quiet this evening. Maggie was turned away from the booth with her feet in the aisle, reading a book called *The Films of James Dean*. The tome was as hefty as an encyclopedia, and the man had starred in only three movies.

Grounded or not, Maggie knew that Mary wouldn't forbid her to read. She'd brought the book along tonight as a sort of protest, and as ineffectual as she felt, Mary had allowed it.

It seemed sometimes to Mary that Maggie was immune to punishment, but what more could she do? She could hardly threaten to take away the ballet lessons—Maggie would jump for joy at that. In fact, Mary wondered just how she herself was going to survive the next four weeks with her daughter, who was usually cranky if she went a single week without seeing *Rebel Without a Cause*.

"More coffee?" their waitress asked.

Mary nodded. Every Thursday night, the same kind woman kept the coffee coming fast and furious, and Mary was grateful for her presence. If it wasn't for the waitress, she feared she would feel like the only talking person on the planet.

Too soon, the waitress was gone again. These nights were always tough on Mary. Even though she tried to think of Thursday as just another night in her busy schedule, it always reminded her that no matter how tightly she planned her life, something seemed to be missing. Sometimes she wondered how it would be to have dinner with someone who was really interested in her conversation. Or just in her.

"I smell smoke!" Mrs. Williamson exclaimed out of the blue.

Maggie's head jerked up. "There's a smoking section right behind us," she replied hastily, nodding in its direction. Clear across the room, the smoking area was deserted.

Mary looked at her daughter and tried to sniff inconspicuously. She had noticed the smell of smoke a lot lately, but she had assumed that it was just a residual odor from the office, where people were allowed to smoke in their offices. Now she realized the awful truth. Her daughter smelled like an ashtray.

Mary felt her shoulders sag another notch. It was bad enough that her daughter's clothes had holes in them and that her hair was still orange. Mary had accepted Maggie's convincing her class to picket life science because they were scheduled to dissect frogs. Sometimes she was even a bit proud that her daughter had such a strong nonconformist streak.

But smoking, she knew, was troubling behavior for a twelve-year-old. Was her daughter about to go completely out of control? Mary had heard of perfectly hardworking, respectable people whose children went berserk with rebellion. And it always started with little things . . . like smoking.

What could she do? Mary rarely thought about Bill Moore, but lately she'd found herself wishing she had someone to confer with, to confide in. She also wished Maggie could have grown up with another role model. Sometimes her daughter seemed like a stranger to her, so different in her interests and aspirations from herself. And though she knew Maggie wasn't mean, at times she sensed a devilry in her daughter that left her completely befuddled.

Just then, as Maggie let out another belabored, audible sigh and shifted in the booth, Mary did likewise, silently and imperceptibly. Maggie would never listen to her—not her own mother, a mere mortal secretary. Nothing would do for Maggie but a full-blown hero, made to order from her twelve-year-old imagination and cut from the same cloth as that oily film star she was so hyper about. Unfortunately, Mary thought with a touch of whimsy, inspirational, law-abiding greasers seemed to be in short supply these days.

On his way home from the hospital, Kyle felt the wind whip against his face and heard a tinny sound as it fell on his helmet. God, he was cold—cold and tired. And he would have sold his soul, he thought as his motorcycle idled at a red light, for a hot cup of coffee.

As he had predicted, Cindy hadn't wanted to eat. She had just wanted to dance the *lambada*. At first, Kyle had been happy to oblige; he'd still been more concerned with the

Jacuzzi than his stomach two hours ago. But then, amidst the bumping and grinding fray of the club, the heel of Cindy's shoe had broken, and Kyle had watched his date spill all over the marble dance floor. The doctor at the emergency room said that she had fractured her coccyx.

The light turned green and Kyle continued down Mockingbird Lane at a sensible rainy-night speed. It was high time he did *something* sensible, he thought. After Cindy was released from the hospital, he was going to have to call it off with her. They had very little in common, and he'd let their flirtation linger on for too long already—maybe because he'd been lonely after his father had died. Or maybe because he wished they were compatible. He wanted a relationship, deep and lasting, something to keep him home on rainy nights. But, obviously, that wasn't going to happen with Cindy.

Up ahead, Kyle spied the Brass Kettle's brightly lit, cheery sign. The restaurant was furnished with ample vinyl booths and was the kind of place where it was okay to take kids. It seemed like years since he'd been there, but he remembered its bland coziness and trustworthy coffee. Impulsively, he turned his bike into the parking lot.

He wasn't as wet as he could have been, Kyle noted as he unfolded himself from the seat and took off his helmet. Anyway, he wasn't likely to see anyone he knew at the Brass Kettle.

The bomber jacket caught her eye, and then the black jeans, seeming even blacker because the guy was wet. She couldn't quite see his face, but she liked the way he slicked back his hair with his hand after he'd pulled off his helmet. What a bike! Now those were wheels.

Maggie continued watching the guy's back as he strolled past the rain-streaked glass windows of the restaurant. Surely he was lost. Or maybe he'd just pulled in for a paper from one of the newspaper boxes that lined the building's entrance. She bet he'd buy one of those strange papers, like the *New York Times*; cool motorcycle guys in bomber jackets just didn't belong on boring old Mockingbird Lane, and they certainly didn't come into the Brass Kettle.

Neither would she, when she was finally old enough to seize control of her own destiny. No, when she was old enough, she planned to hop on a motorcycle just like the one parked outside and head for somewhere exciting, like Mexico, or Canada, or at least Fort Worth.

Although staring wasn't kosher, Maggie found herself craning her neck as the stranger appeared inside the restaurant's glass doors. She couldn't believe it. The cool leather guy was coming into this dump? He wasn't going to sit at one of the stools at the counter, either. He was heading right toward them, to take his place in one of the geeky booths.

She cast her eyes toward her book and watched him on the sly, not wanting to be caught staring like a jerk. But then she saw something weird. The guy had a paper all right—the *Wall Street Journal*. And there was something strange about him, or not strange. Familiar. She knew this guy.

Just as he came even with the booth, their eyes met. Maggie's head snapped up, and she bit her lip to keep from gasping. This guy—this hip motorcycle dude—was Kyle Weston! The suit she'd met this very afternoon. Her mom's boss.

Dad.

A million conflicting thoughts raced through her mind. He had slicked-back hair and the jacket of her dreams. Why was he reading that gross newspaper? He was her father, her dream dad, in the flesh. But this afternoon he'd seemed such a loser. Now... She stared into his matinee-idol brown eyes and feared she was going to faint.

"Maggie?" he asked.

Mary jumped. In her Thursday-night funk, she hadn't even noticed anyone approaching the table. The vinyl of the booth made a squeaky sound as she turned and looked at the man who had spoken to her daughter.

"Kyle? I mean, Mr. Weston?"

"Mary, hi!" His eyes twinkled with surprise at the chance meeting.

"What are you doing here?" Mary asked before she could think twice.

Kyle shrugged. "Came for some coffee and maybe a burger." He glanced around the restaurant. "Do you mind if I join you?"

"Oh—" Mary hesitated. She really hadn't planned on this.

"Have a seat," Maggie said quickly, scooting farther into the booth to make room.

Kyle took up Maggie's offer before Mary could nix it, which she'd appeared about to do. Really, he hadn't meant to impose himself, but he would have felt even more awkward sitting by himself a few seats away from them.

Once seated, he found himself across from an elderly woman, who was staring at him curiously. He held out his hand. "My name's Kyle Weston."

"Who?" the woman asked, addressing the question to Mary.

"Mr. Weston, my boss," she explained, leaning close to the woman's ear and almost shouting.

"Oh!" The woman glanced at Kyle again, then appeared perplexed. "I thought you died." The words were said so loudly that the occupants of several tables turned to look.

The color completely drained from Mary's face. "Oh, Mrs. Williamson, no—"

Kyle smiled. "That was my father. He passed away several weeks ago. It's nice to meet you, Mrs. Williamson."

"Is that really your motorcycle?" Maggie asked, pointing out the window.

"Yeah, it is," Kyle answered.

"That's just the kind I'm gonna get."

"They'll probably have better bikes by the time you're old enough to buy one."

He hadn't laughed, or told her that girls didn't ride motorcycles, or given her a safety lecture. Maggie nearly swooned. How had she ever doubted that this guy was her father?

Mary wondered at Maggie's odd behavior. First she invited a near stranger—an authority figure, almost—to join them, and now she couldn't stop gaping at the poor man.

Of course, Mary was having a hard time taking her eyes off him herself. The leather jacket, the item she was sure had captured Maggie's fancy, did lend him a certain dazzle. In his casual clothes, and away from the fluorescent lights and standard-issue office furniture of the agency, Kyle appeared tanner, more rugged—more intimidating.

She didn't know if she really wanted to be across from this man for the next hour. "Don't feel obligated to sit with us," she said. "We wouldn't want to detain you."

"Detain me?" Kyle asked. "I just got here."

Mary felt herself blush a little, but she soldiered on. "I meant, I know you have other plans..." Her unfinished sentence clearly implied that she wondered what had happened to his date.

Kyle leaned back and crossed his arms. "Something came up." Someone went down was more like it, but he wasn't going to sit here in front of prim, mature Mary and talk about the night's dancing fiasco. Luckily, the waitress came at that moment to deliver the three dinners and took his order.

"I like your jacket, too," Maggie said.

"Thanks," Kyle answered.

Again, Mary forced herself to take a hard look at the offending article. She really couldn't see anything spectacular in the supple, worn leather, except that Kyle did seem rather dashing in it—or was it just the wearer who created that impression? She caught herself staring at Kyle's chest and looked quickly to his face to see if he had noticed. His brown eyes glinted with humor.

"I want one just like it," Maggie was saying, "but Mom says they make people look like hoodlums."

Blood rushed into Mary's cheeks. "Maggie..."

Kyle nearly choked on his coffee. He glanced at Mary's beet-red face and then turned to her daughter. "I think she meant that at your age, it might seem a little...ostentatious."

Maggie's eyes widened, and then she blinked. Ostentatious? She didn't know what it meant, but it didn't sound good. "Do you think so, too?" she asked.

From the blank look on her face, Kyle could tell Maggie didn't have the faintest idea of what he was talking about. "I think she might have a point."

That didn't sit well with Maggie, but coming from someone as cool as Kyle Weston, defeat wasn't so hard to accept. Only, she worried that he didn't see what kindred spirits they were. "I'll probably get one when I'm older, though," she pronounced. "Just before I blow this Popsicle stand."

"What?" Kyle asked.

"Before she leaves Dallas," Mary translated.

"Oh." Kyle nodded. He could sympathize with the girl's dreams of moving on to better things, but it wasn't a topic he felt like taking up. Not with Mary sitting two feet away. He took another swig of coffee and watched Mary. She looked especially pretty in a teal-green knit dress. She'd never worn it to the office.

"She won't let me cut my hair like James Dean's, either," Maggie persisted.

Kyle bit back a smile. "That is rough."

"Your hair is beautiful, Maggie. You don't want to give it a Mohawk."

"James Dean never had a Mohawk, Mom!" Maggie said, rolling her eyes.

Kyle laughed. "But those curls of yours might not behave in a ducktail."

He knew what James Dean's hair looked like. He understood her, right down to her tormented soul, she knew he did. Only, Kyle didn't seem to be too interested in her. He kept looking at her mother. They were scoping each other out, all right. It was annoying.

She bowed her head and scowled dramatically. "Someday I'm gonna get a crew cut."

The words were meant to shock, but Kyle just chuckled. "Or you could just shave it all off, and really make a statement," he suggested with a sly wink toward her mother.

He was making fun of her, but Maggie decided that he was really doing it for her mom's sake. When she thought about it rationally, it was a good thing that he was so interested in her mother, since he was her father. Wasn't that what she wanted—the three of them, together? After they got things straightened out, all the attention would be focused on her again. And Kyle probably would be more lenient. Compared to moms, dads were all pushovers.

Under Kyle's persistent gaze, it was all Mary could do to concentrate on her club sandwich. If she wasn't mistaken, that was male appreciation in his eyes...but she must be mistaken. She knew the kind of women Kyle liked, or she could imagine. They certainly weren't the kind of women who skimped on frivolities and whose big night out was dinner at the Brass Kettle. Frankly, she was surprised to see Kyle in this place.

"Do you come here often?" she asked, nearly laughing at how silly the words sounded once they were out. If they hadn't been in such innocuous surroundings, her question would have sounded like a pickup line. But then, Kyle Weston was probably plenty used to receiving those anywhere.

"Not recently," Kyle answered honestly. "I used to, but . . ." Kyle didn't know how to finish the sentence. It was hard to explain when the idea of simply nursing a cup of coffee at a diner had become alien to his life-style. Sitting here with Mary and her little tribe suddenly made him feel ridiculous for ever wanting anything else, or more.

Mary nodded, filling in the blank left by his silence. *But he had more exciting ways to spend his time.* Kyle was just slumming here.

"What does your boyfriend do for a living, Mary?" Mrs. Williamson asked.

Kyle grinned, but Mary was horrified. "Mrs. Williamson, Mr. Weston is my *boss,*" she said loudly. Again, the surrounding tables swung around for a look.

"I worked at Murry's Drugs for twenty years," Mrs. Williamson announced, "and my boss never took me out to dinner."

"Oh, well, Mr. Weston just happened to be here."

Ignoring Mary's protest, Mrs. Williamson looked up from her split pea soup to study Kyle. "You must like Mary a whole lot if you're willing to get wet just to eat a hamburger with her."

Mary sighed, knowing she was licked. She shot Kyle an apologetic glance. "We eat here every Thursday," she explained.

"Just Thursday?" Kyle asked, curious.

"Well, every other night is taken. I volunteer most evenings, except Monday, which is PTA night. My church group runs a soup kitchen, and then on Tuesdays I play bridge with a neighborhood group. Saturdays I work at the hospital, except this Saturday there's a picnic.''

"At the hospital?'' Kyle asked, a little overwhelmed by her schedule. He'd started losing track after the Monday PTA meetings.

"No, there's a Friends of the Public Library annual picnic this weekend. Maggie volunteers for them after school, so I try to go. People donate books, and the library sells some of their overstock.''

"Mother,'' Maggie moaned. "You're putting us all to sleep.''

"Hardly,'' Kyle countered. He kept his focus on Mary. How had he forgotten how pretty she was? An idea struck him. "You say the library needs books? My father left a ton of books that I need to get rid of.''

"It's a good time to donate,'' Mary said a little breathlessly. Between them, she could feel a little current of attraction. And now he was angling to see her again, outside of work. She knew it was wrong, but she felt a little flutter in her stomach. Even if it was just a public library picnic.

"I could bring them down, maybe pack a lunch,'' Kyle was saying. "And then Saturday night...''

Night? Mary wondered. It sounded as if he wanted to turn the innocent little picnic into something like a date. That couldn't happen.

"You can't do that,'' she blurted out suddenly, interrupting whatever plans he was hashing out.

"Why not?'' he asked, startled.

"Because—'' She searched frantically for a reason, then found it. "Because you're going on a business trip this weekend.''

He rolled his eyes. "Of course. How could I forget?''

"I don't know,'' Mary said stiffly, glad she had averted danger. She could not start hoping to see Kyle Weston outside the office. Especially not now that she'd discovered she still found him attractive.

A phrase she'd written in her diary years ago came back to her. "I'm so besotted I'm numb," were the words she'd put down for posterity. But she wouldn't let that happen again. She had too many responsibilities in her life to afford to be besotted or numb.

"I suppose it's a good thing your secretary was around to jog your memory," she said.

Mary said the word "secretary" very formally, as if to remind them of their real relationship. Kyle scowled. "Yeah, well, I guess the library accepts donations at other times."

"All year long," Maggie said in exasperation. "Then we have to fix them up and put them on the shelves. Have you ever actually thought about the poor people who have to rubber cement those card holders in the backs of books? I'd rather throw a party for people who didn't donate books."

"Maggie!"

Kyle smiled again, glad for the excuse to cover his disappointment. But Mary was probably right to be wary. He didn't make a habit of socializing with employees, especially women. Especially the clerical staff. And in Mary's case, especially her.

"Well, I can see you have an active life outside the office."

"Zieglar and Weston is still my first priority," Mary said cautiously.

"I wish I had so many irons in the fire," Kyle admitted. "It seems as if I'm always making up things for myself to do and not really attending to the things I really care about."

"Really?" Mary asked, surprised. "That's not how it seems to me."

Kyle's eyebrow rose quizzically.

"I mean, you always seem to have...companions," Mary said awkwardly.

Kyle was glad the waitress chose that moment to bring his hamburger and refill the coffee cups. He asked Mary more about her volunteer work, and chewed thoughtfully while she spoke.

"Geez, Mother," Maggie said finally, pushing away her half-eaten grilled cheese sandwich. "You sure are talking a lot."

Kyle laughed, and Mary ducked her head, blushing. "I guess I am," she apologized.

"I've enjoyed myself," Kyle said. Too much, he thought. Even given the awkwardness of the chance meeting, he couldn't remember when he'd felt more relaxed. Why, in the span of one hour he'd gone from *lambada* disaster to volunteering to attend a civic picnic—and feeling actual disappointment that he couldn't attend.

He had probably been under too much stress lately, he told himself. After a sunny weekend in California, he'd forget all about this little domestic scene and be able to tackle his work and jazz up his private life again. And he'd probably forget all about Mary and her kid, and how much he'd enjoyed hanging out with them. It was pointless to dwell on, at any rate.

Kyle took a deep breath and glanced at his watch. "Well, I'd better go," he said, throwing his napkin down by his plate. "It was nice running into you all."

"You're leaving?" Maggie asked.

"Maggie, Mr. Weston probably has somewhere to go."

"Not really," Kyle corrected, "but I do have an early flight." They all got up and left the restaurant together after Mrs. Williamson had gathered a doggie bag for Fritz, her poodle.

"It's stopped raining," Mary said as they gathered around her car. Maggie and Mrs. Williamson got in.

"Too late for me, I'm afraid." He was still damp from his foolhardy motorcycle escapade.

"I hope you don't catch cold before your trip," Mary said. She glanced toward the passengers in the car's interior and added, "and I hope you'll understand Mrs. Williamson didn't mean—"

Kyle waved off her explanation. "I do. She's a nice woman. She just needs a new hearing aid."

"Really?" Mary asked. "She has one, but she never wears it."

"It probably doesn't fit right—or she doesn't know how to adjust it. My dad had the same difficulty. You should try to convince her to see her ear doctor."

Mary nodded. "Thanks, I'll try." She got into the car and said goodbye through the driver's window.

"Good night, Mary," Kyle replied. He watched her drive away, surprised to feel something like regret.

She was still so beautiful. Not that beauty was the be-all and end-all, but he couldn't seem to get her image out of his mind. It had been nice to see her laugh tonight, too. If nothing else, the night had been successful as a comparison study. First had been the disastrous date, then a taste of what life might have been like if he hadn't wasted all this time.

Kyle froze, then slowly got on his bike. Had the last thirteen years of his life really been a waste? He liked being a . . . well, a playboy. There was nothing shameful in that. Weren't people supposed to sow their wild oats? And was it his fault that Mary had been ready to settle down before he was? Now that he thought about it, he'd done them both a big favor by breaking it off when he did. His decision had probably saved them a lot of conflict and grief.

He felt a pang of guilt. Mary had been a virgin before he met her—he hadn't had the courtesy of breaking off their relationship before he'd taken that from her. He wondered if she regretted sleeping with him. Maybe she had felt guilty herself, or perhaps she had been sowing some wild oats, too—that once with him—before settling down to marry that other guy.

Most likely, it would all remain a mystery. Anyway, Mary Moore's life wasn't really any of his business now. He had to put her out of his mind, once and for all.

"'Night, Maggie."

Maggie grunted a response and flopped over beneath the covers. She listened to her mother's retreating footsteps and the closing of her bedroom door. And then she let out the biggest sigh of her lifetime.

What a day. It had been touch and go there for a few hours, but it looked like she'd found the appropriate father. Her only problem now was that he didn't know it.

And he hadn't seemed too impressed with her, now that she thought about it. But then, Maggie supposed that grown-ups paid as little attention to kids as vice versa. Until those grown-ups realized that the kids belonged to them. Kyle obviously didn't know he had a daughter. When he did, he would appreciate her finer qualities.

Which presented her with a whole new problem. How was she going to let him know?

Down the hall, lying in her own bed, Mary tried to think of all the things she could accomplish in the coming week. She'd broached the idea of a new hearing aid to Mrs. Williamson, so she would set up an appointment on Saturday for her. She was amazed at how insightful Kyle had been after being around the woman for only an hour.

Kyle! She had to stop thinking about him. After a few uncomfortable weeks and one dinner, she was stuck in the rut she'd avoided for thirteen years. In her thirty-four years, Kyle Weston had been the one weakness she'd allowed herself, and even that had been a terrible mistake.

When she was twenty-one and had just landed her job at Zieglar and Weston after finishing secretarial college, the world had seemed to be just how she wanted it. After growing up in the poorest section of town with a wisecracking handyman for a father, she knew she wanted a more steady, sober life for herself.

Zieglar and Weston was recommended to her by her young accounting professor, Bill Moore. Bill had a crush on her, and had even hinted that he wanted to marry her. Although she liked him, Mary hadn't been all that interested. Even though she was the most practical person she knew, always wanting to be the little fish in the big pond, deep down inside she secretly harbored dreams of meeting a man who would set her pulse racing. Nice as he was, Bill Moore just wasn't the racing-pulses type.

Kyle Weston was. Young, handsome, clearly on the way to the top of the company, he came on the scene like an Adonis in her workaday life. He'd just finished college at one of the Ivy Leagues, and as an intern—albeit a special one—there was nothing untoward in his socializing with the lower-ranking members of the staff. He even took Mary out a few times, and although she knew that someone like Kyle Weston would never be interested in her, that autumn she'd developed a crush on him. By Christmas, the crush had blossomed into a full-blown case of unrequited love.

It wasn't just that he was handsome. He was the type of person she'd never had much contact with. In high school, boys like Kyle had played sports and joined the debating team, while Mary had found her home in activities like biology club and choir. She would never have thought that she'd have anything in common with a man like Kyle Weston, but she did.

That fall, she laughed more than she had in the first twenty years of her life. Sometimes they simply talked about what they wanted for their futures and what they thought of the world around them. Although Kyle was confident and brash, his manner was often good-naturedly self-deprecating, and at times he expressed bitterness about being soldiered about by his father. Mary always scolded him for this. With or without his father, it was obvious that Kyle Weston would be successful in whatever he wanted.

And sometime around Christmas, he started wanting her. She sensed it in the way he would look at her with those incredible dark eyes and the way he managed to touch her in some way whenever they met, even if they were just passing in the halls of Zieglar and Weston. As much as she wanted him, Mary had held back. It just didn't seem practical to fall for a playboy-in-the-making like Kyle.

At the company Christmas party that year, though, he had been at his most dazzling. He'd charmed the socks off everyone, dancing with the secretaries and sharing drinks with his office buddies. With a champagne bottle in one hand and a sprig of mistletoe in the other, he was good cheer personified. Although he didn't say much to Mary, she sensed him watching her. Their gazes met ever more frequently across the crowded meeting room as the afternoon progressed, and at quitting time it just seemed natural that they should leave together.

They drove through Dallas's winter drizzle, which seemed to Mary as romantic as a full-fledged white Christmas. It seemed to be understood that they would end the evening at Kyle's place—a garage apartment in Highland Park that was more spacious than the house she had grown up in. For one night, she promised herself, she would enjoy the comforts of the privileged and let herself feel the privilege of being loved.

And she did. All night, Kyle awakened her to sensations previously unknown to her. He was gentle and caring, but at the same time insistent. Mary had never even seen a man naked before—never had a man see her body unclothed, either—but Kyle made their sharing of each other seem the most natural and undeniable thing in the world.

Was it any wonder that she woke the next morning filled with a dream of never having to leave his side? she asked herself now for the thousandth time. Perhaps her mistake had been expressing her feelings aloud.

On the drive home, after she'd confessed how she felt, Kyle had practically run his car off the road. In the broad light of day, as he explained that the passion of the night before could never be repeated, Mary had seen the panic in his eyes—the panic of being trapped for life with someone like her.

"You're too serious," he'd explained, concentrating on the road to avoid looking at her.

"You didn't say anything about that last night," Mary said, wishing she didn't feel the need to defend herself, her feelings and the fact that she was in love with him.

"Damn!" He screeched the car around a tight corner. "I'm sorry, Mary. But you've said yourself that I'm a jerk. I'm just not ready for a serious commitment. That's what you want, isn't it?"

Mary nodded miserably. She'd never felt like such a drab nobody in her life. But was it unrealistic or wrong to want a lasting relationship—even with somebody who was pulses-racing good-looking? Apparently, though, it wasn't going to happen, and she felt incredibly foolish. Men like Kyle Weston didn't marry secretaries. She'd known that all along. And yet she'd run right into his snare.

"You deserve better than me, anyway," Kyle said as he pulled into her parents' drive, letting the car idle.

Her mortification finally turning to indignation, Mary scowled and reached for the door handle. "If it makes you feel better to say that, go ahead. But what you really mean is the exact opposite. I'm just a little peon to you, aren't I?"

She watched his face go ghostly pale and smirked triumphantly. "Don't worry," she said, "I won't bug you again. This has been just as much my fault as yours. Come the New

Year, you can seduce somebody else with a clear conscience."

Mary stepped out of the car and was about to shut the door when Kyle called to her to wait. For a moment, her heart skipped a beat. Maybe he'd changed his mind, she thought as she leaned in to hear what he had to say.

"Are you going to be okay with your folks?" he asked.

"Of course," she lied. "I am an adult." With that, she slammed the door shut and headed up the driveway, diverting herself by trying to think up excuses for having spent the night out. And she'd been trying to make up excuses for that night for thirteen years now.

The following week, Mary had been convinced that she would have gone over the deep end were it not for Bill Moore. They'd been seeing each other steadily since she had left school, and even sporadically after she'd become obsessed with Kyle. Now, after her flight of fancy, Bill's stick-to-itiveness looked more attractive than ever.

They eloped on January third, and when she came back to the office after their brief honeymoon, Kyle had gone to California. Then, a few weeks later, Mary found herself pregnant. Finally, she'd thought, her life was her own. She had a man who loved her, and she'd always wanted a child. Being realistic had its advantages.

But true reality set in three months later, when Bill died in a car accident coming home from work one evening. She had a baby on the way, very little money and more time to worry about both than she could deal with. That was when her life of volunteerism had started. She threw herself into any activity that would blot out the memory of Bill, Kyle and the series of events that had changed her life forever in a few short months.

And now, Mary decided as she tossed under the comforter, she would have to do the same thing again, and reinforce the diligent avoidance she'd practiced for the past thirteen years. Otherwise, she would be headed for disaster again. And this time, she wouldn't have Bill Moore to bail her out.

She did have Maggie, though. Her daughter needed her full attention right now. Throwing herself into mother overdrive would not only benefit her relationship with Maggie, it would keep her from dwelling on Kyle. Yes, she thought, with extra diligence, she could keep her mind off Kyle.

Yet, as she drifted into a troubled sleep, her mind kept replaying how Kyle had looked, sitting across the table from her, talking to Maggie, smiling, listening, laughing. Memories of thirteen years ago milled and mixed with the present, creating a disturbing jumble of impressions. And every once in a while, Maggie would appear in her dreams, sometimes with Bill Moore, the father she never knew, and then, once, with Kyle.

Mary woke up in a cold sweat. She was going insane, she was sure of it. Or maybe she was just being forced to face what she had denied for so long....

Chapter Three

The first thing he was going to do when he got home was call Cindy, Kyle thought as he paid the parking attendant at the Dallas-Fort Worth airport. So she wasn't perfect. Tonight, even though it was only Monday, he just needed to cut loose.

All weekend he'd daydreamed about Mary. During his Saturday meeting, when he should have been focusing on the serious business of trying to merge his own small company with Zieglar and Weston, all he could think about was that damn picnic. Then he kept imagining Mary and Maggie puttering around their house, doing weekend things like eating pancakes and watching television together—perfect little homey scenes.

He couldn't go on like this. Thirty-five was too old to develop the urge to nest. Maybe his father had been right, and he should have settled down a long time ago. It would have saved him from these inconvenient, spontaneous domestic compulsions. They were surely just a sign of age.

Cindy was the antidote to this problem. They could do something date-ish, like go to a movie; he always made it a point to take her someplace where they didn't have to talk too much. Conversation with Cindy was a little like having *People* magazine read aloud on cassette. The woman lived for gossip.

He had always enjoyed talking to Mary, he thought as he pulled off the expressway. He remembered the conversations they'd had when they were young, although he'd probably done most of the talking back then. But Mary was always a great listener, and she never failed to give good advice.

Cindy, he reminded himself. Cindy was the one he was interested in. Cindy was fun, in her own way. And she wasn't his secretary, or the woman he had jilted over a decade before. What did he and Mary have in common, anyway? She probably didn't even have time to go out to dinner, or to the movies, or dan—

Cindy. Kyle let out a sigh as he pulled into his driveway. His salvation was in the hospital with a fractured tailbone.

"Howdy, neighbor!" Sam Terry called. He turned off his lawn mower and came over to Kyle's car.

"Little early yet to start mowing, isn't it, Sam?" Kyle asked, hauling his suitcase out of the trunk.

"Can't let these things get out of hand," Sam explained. "Good way to get air, too."

Good way to get a lungful of dirt and grass, Kyle thought. It was March, and although it was warmer, the grass hadn't begun to take off as it would in another month. He couldn't imagine going out of his way to mow before absolutely necessary.

That's what marriage does to a person, a little voice inside him warned.

"Say, Sam..." Kyle began.

"Yeah?"

"Did you ever, you know, do yard work when you were a bachelor?"

"Me?" Sam looked shocked. "Ask me another one. Man, what I wouldn't do for the good old days. Why, me and my friends, we used to go out and—"

"That's all I wanted to know."

"Yeah, well, nobody has to explain these things to you, bud. Why, I just happened to be looking out the window the other night and saw one of your conquests staking out your house. Almost came down and told her you were away for the weekend, but I didn't want to rub salt in the poor thing's wounds."

"A woman?" Kyle asked. "At my house?" It couldn't have been Cindy, that was for sure.

"Cute little brunette," Sam elaborated. "'Course, I couldn't tell much more than that, seeing how it was dark."

Kyle thought for a moment. "That's strange."

"Well, moths to the flame, I guess. They just flock to you, even when you're not here. She left you a love note, though."

"A note?" Kyle asked. "Where?"

"I saw her pin it to your side door," Sam explained. "I didn't read it."

"Of course not." Kyle shut his car door and started moving toward the side yard.

"Oh, hey, buddy?"

Kyle turned back to Sam. "Yeah?"

"You might want to give your azaleas a hit of water every once in a while. They're looking a little peaked."

"Sure thing, Sam." Kyle waited until his neighbor went back to his side of the hedge, then shook his head. Marriage created monsters, it seemed. And Sam was supposedly happily married.

As he reached the side door, Kyle saw that there indeed was a note there. He tore it down and glanced quickly at the several pages. There was no signature anywhere, nor did the pages appear to be addressed to him. He studied them more intently. The four pages—journal entries dated over a decade earlier—were photocopies. What the hell was this?

Then a snatch of the neat loopy handwriting caught his eye, and he understood. The entry was dated December 24.

This has to be the worst day of my life. For months I've been wondering whether K.W. really likes me, and now I know. Not only does he not love me, after last night, he probably despises me. I feel like a fool, but I can't forget what it felt like to have his hands on my body. I'll never forget. I'm so besotted I'm numb...

Mary's diary. Kyle felt his face burning, and he promptly folded the pages. He couldn't imagine how these pages wound up on his door, but he shouldn't be reading them. Those were private thoughts, never intended for his eyes.

However, as he puttered around his kitchen fixing coffee after laying the photocopies carefully on the breakfast table, he found the temptation to peek at them just once more unbearable. Fifteen minutes later, he was ensconced in an easy chair with a steaming mug in one hand. In the other he held Mary's diary pages. The words completely absorbed him.

December 25: Merry Christmas? I've never felt so miserable! Why did I ever mention the word "marriage" to K.W.? If I hadn't, we might still be seeing each other. I can't believe I'm such a dope...

Then, later:

B. came over today. For Christmas, he changed the oil in my car, but we were gabbing while he worked and he ended up putting too much in. I'm taking the car to the mechanic tomorrow. Poor B. When I refused to let him pay, he asked me to marry him. I said no thanks, and he said he'd ask again next week. He's so nice, I wish I was in love with him. But then, who needs love when you can have somebody who'll mess up your car for free?

Kyle sank lower into his chair. How could he have just left her like that, to run off and marry somebody she didn't love? But if she married the guy, one part of his brain countered, could she really have been as in love as she thought she was? That thought didn't sit well with him, either, and he wondered at the perverse little demon inside of him that actually wanted to believe Mary had carried a torch for him into her brief marriage. He was a heel, plain and simple.

As if to confirm this thought, on the last page, one passage in particular caught his attention.

As promised, B. asked me again. I told him I'd think about it. Meanwhile, I've been worrying, worrying, worrying. Today I actually went to the library to look up female reproduction. Boy, did I feel like an idiot! I think K.W. used something—but what if it didn't work? Time will tell, I guess.

He felt like a worm. Never once had he called to ask if she was okay. Instead, he'd left her to work through everything alone. At least she'd had that other guy, he thought. At least things had come out all right.

Through the night, he returned to the pages again and again. The raw emotion they revealed tore at him. No wonder Mary didn't want to have anything to do with him now—outside of their barely tolerable professional relationship. But if that was the case, the little demon asked, why did she go to the trouble of putting her diary on his door?

That was the real puzzler. Perhaps she wanted to show him, without actually having to discuss the matter, why she felt this way. Or maybe... maybe she was still in love with him.

All night long, Kyle veered back and forth from one supposition to another. Each time he got out of bed, restless, to fetch a magazine or a drink of water—anything to take his mind off that diary—his curiosity about Mary's motives only grew stronger. By morning, when he woke bleary-eyed and dog-tired, his frustration had taken on a certain self-righteousness.

He deserved to know the truth. She couldn't just leave him like this, with his not knowing whether those pages were a reprimand or a kindly reminder. And he would find out which they were—today—from the horse's mouth.

Hectic was the only word to describe that morning at the office. The place was abuzz with activity, thanks to Canine Gourmet Dog Dinners.

"Mr. Hadley is quite upset," Mary said the moment Kyle walked in the door. "He wants a conference call."

Even in his cranky, caffeine-deprived state, Kyle watched Mary closely, noting that she didn't look the least bit embarrassed or guilty. Well, he couldn't just come right out and ask her about the diary in front of the entire staff. But she was bound to crack at some point in the day. He'd make sure of it.

He drummed his fingers on his desk. "Did you transfer him to Sykes?" he asked.

"Yes," Mary replied, "but it wasn't the graphics that bothered Mr. Hadley. He said he'd decided that he didn't like the concept of giving away free flea collars with dog food."

"But we talked about this!" Kyle snapped. Mary's eyes widened, but she appeared to take his foul temper in stride. He made an effort to lower his voice. "I thought we were in agreement on the flea collars."

Mary organized a conference call between Kyle, Sykes and Hadley, and stayed in Kyle's office to take notes. It turned out that Hadley, CEO of Canine Gourmet, Inc., had begun to suspect that offering flea collars would give consumers the idea that Canine Gourmet Dog Dinners caused fleas.

"Now, what I was thinking," Hadley said in his monotonous drawl through the speakerphone, "was that we could do approximately the same ad, substituting squeaky toys for flea collars."

Kyle watched Sykes and Mary exchange amused glances. How could Mary behave so casually today? Didn't she care that he had read her most personal thoughts, even if they were thirteen years old? He couldn't think of anything else. And worse, she didn't appear to have lost any sleep over the matter. She seemed her efficient, competent self—only more so, because he himself felt like a wreck.

"Weston?" the disembodied voice said.

Sykes cleared his throat and Kyle bolted to attention. He had to get a grip. "Yes, Mr. Hadley... I'm right with you. Uh, how did you come up with this squeaky toy idea?"

"Well, my youngest, Amy, has a dog named Peaches. And she says Peaches would much rather..."

Kyle watched Mary smooth her blue skirt over her knees. Was that a nervous gesture? She didn't look particularly nervous. She looked... attractive. Well rested. Not like a woman with a guilty conscience. Maybe she wasn't going to crack, after all. He simply had to speak with her today.

"Uh, Kyle?"

When Kyle pulled his gaze away from Mary's shapely knee, two sets of eyes were peering expectantly at him. Sykes nodded pointedly toward the speakerphone.

"Oh," Kyle said. Damn that woman! How was he supposed to concentrate when she had filled his head with all sorts of troubling questions? Now he'd completely lost track of Hadley's conversation.

"Well, Mr. Hadley," he improvised, hoping that his comment wouldn't be completely off the mark, "I imagine that Peaches knows better than any of us what kind of giveaway a dog would want."

The machine on his desk chuckled, as did Mary and Sykes. "That's so. He's a cocker spaniel, you know."

"The only problem I see," Kyle explained, "is that we had planned the campaign around the health angle. There's not much healthy about a squeaking piece of rubber."

"Oh." Hadley sounded worried. "Well, you folks could always just jiggle around with the slogan a bit. You know, instead of 'A Healthy Dog Is a Happy Dog,' say, 'A Happy Dog Is a Healthy Dog.'"

"Mmm." The room was silent. Kyle was gratified to note that Mary and Sykes looked about as confused as he felt. "Why don't I run your idea by Mr. Zieglar and get back to you?"

"Okeydoke," Hadley said and hung up.

Kyle leaned back in his leather chair and let out a sigh. "Sometimes I wonder if I'm cut out for this."

"Maybe you could retire," Ben Sykes said, "and we could change the name of the company to Zieglar and Peaches."

"Very funny," Kyle muttered. "Although it does seem as if the dogs are running this particular show."

"Are you feeling all right, Mr. Weston?" Mary asked.

Kyle jerked himself up straight. The concern in Mary's voice sounded genuine, which only made him more suspicious. "Why?" he asked. "Don't I look all right?"

"Well..." Mary hesitated. What was the matter with him today? She'd never seen Kyle so frayed at the edges. "Actually, no. You look pale."

"I wonder why," Kyle said, reclining in his chair again. He sent Mary a piercing stare over his steepled fingers. In response, she appeared to fidget uncomfortably. Good. Now they were getting somewhere.

"Maybe you haven't had enough rest," she said in a low voice.

"Ah!" Kyle leaned forward. "But why? Do you think it's something in the air? How have you been sleeping, Mary?"

Mary felt herself blush. His use of her first name sounded sarcastic. If she didn't know better, she'd think that he was mad at her for something. But what could she have done wrong? "Fine," she said finally, her voice barely a whisper. "I'm just fine."

Kyle continued to stare at her after she had averted her eyes. Moments later, he heard Sykes clear his throat again, breaking the tense silence.

"Well, I know I won't get much sleep until this campaign is set in stone," Ben put in, glancing from one to the other. "I say we run it by Zieglar and hash out some new ideas ASAP."

"You're right," Kyle said. He'd have to get back to the matter with Mary. As he got up to leave, he turned to her. "Mary, I need to talk to you later."

Her eyes looked questioningly into his. "Is it anything serious?" she asked.

"What do *you* think?" Kyle asked, then turned and left.

For the rest of the day, Mary worked cautiously at her desk, racking her brain to find some reason for Kyle's odd behavior. And to think that she had come to work determined to think about the man as little as possible. All weekend, she'd scolded herself for mentally rehashing memories best left forgotten.

She had expected that Kyle would have plenty for her to do after his business trip, but oddly enough, he stopped by her desk only once, making a special trip during the meeting in Zieglar's office.

"I need you to send some flowers for me," Kyle said. "They need to go to Parkland Hospital."

"All right," Mary replied. "To whom?"

"Cindy Sellars," Kyle announced. He let the name hover in the air for a moment before adding, "She's my girlfriend."

This was hardly late-breaking news to Mary, yet Kyle had made the pronouncement as if he was playing the chorus in a Greek tragedy. Surely this wasn't the serious matter he'd wanted to talk to her about. But by the arch of his brow, she could tell he was baiting her for a response.

Well, she wasn't nibbling. "Is there anything else?" she asked, keeping her expression impassive. "A message, perhaps?"

His gaze never left her face, but a little smirk touched his lips before he answered, "Just say, 'I'm glad to be the man you fell for,' and sign it with my name."

To her irritation, Mary felt her hand shaking as she jotted down the intimate little message, her handwriting a scrawl against the yellow legal pad. Was Kyle trying to torture her? she wondered as she listened to his retreating footsteps. But then, how could he be, when he had no idea how she felt about him. When *she* didn't even know. Still, he gave every indication of trying to make her jealous—or just plain angry.

She called the order in and found herself disliking Cindy Sellars intensely. The woman was probably young and drop-dead beautiful, as well as footloose and fancy-free—just the way Kyle liked them.

Mary felt a blush of shame creep into her face at her mental tirade. What did she care about Cindy Sellars? Kyle's grizzly-bear mood had her completely off balance. She had Maggie, and a busier life than she could handle sometimes. She certainly didn't need Kyle. Youth tended to be a leveler, and if they hadn't been able to come to an understanding thirteen years ago, they were probably even more hopelessly mismatched now.

She just couldn't go on like this, though. Whatever cat-and-mouse game Kyle was trying to play had to be put to an end, and it was obviously up to her to do it.

When Kyle came out of Zieglar's office again, the meeting apparently ended, Mary fell into step behind him. At his office doorway she hesitated only briefly. He'd said he'd wanted to talk to her; well, she wasn't going to sit around and wait for a summons. She rapped on the doorjamb.

"Yes?" Kyle looked up across his desk, where he had just seated himself. His eyes flashed with speculation upon seeing her, and again Mary got the idea that he was up to something.

Gathering her courage, she stepped in and closed the door behind her. "I need to speak to you," she said, coming to a stop in front of his desk. She didn't make a move to sit, preferring to tower over him for once.

Kyle grinned. "I figured I'd see you in here sometime today."

"Oh?" Mary didn't like the implication of his words—as though she'd just fallen into a trap. "Mr. Weston—"

"Kyle." He smiled again and waited while Mary shifted uncomfortably. "Now what can I help you with?"

"*Help* me?" Mary laughed. "That seems to be the last thing you're interested in. All day you've gone out of your

way to make me feel uncomfortable here. You were the one
who said—''

Kyle stood, zooming in on her accusation and throwing
it back at her. ''I've made you uncomfortable?'' he asked.
''How?''

''By—'' Come to think of it, she didn't know how to answer that question. It wasn't so much what he did, but the
vibes he was sending. Vibes didn't make much of an argument, though. ''You seem to be upset with me,'' she said,
her chin lifting a notch. ''If you don't like my work, I wish
you'd tell me.''

Kyle continued to watch her and nodded thoughtfully.
''This has been difficult for you, hasn't it?''

''What are you talking about?''

''Working for me. After all these years.'' He came around
the desk to stand beside her.

''I—'' Mary felt a blush rise to her face. Lying just wasn't
her forte. ''Well, yes.''

''That's understandable,'' Kyle said. ''And I suppose it's
natural that, in your uneasiness, you would resort to playing games.''

Mary's head snapped up, her eyes wide. ''You're accusing me of playing games? *Me?*'' She couldn't believe the
nerve of the man! ''You've been stalking around this place
all day trying to get a rise out of me!''

''Me?'' he asked. The genuine look of innocence he wore
only made her angrier.

''You know you have! Do you want me to quit?'' She
couldn't believe she was even suggesting such a thing. Maggie's welfare and her own depended on this job. She felt
tears well up in her eyes and shook her head to hold them at
bay.

''No, I don't.''

"Well, you could have fooled me," she huffed. She crossed her arms, reining in control. "If you do, just say so."

"Is that what you want?"

"No!" Feeling as close to the edge as she had been in years, Mary took a step forward. "I just want to do my work," she said, "and not be made to feel as though I've created some federal offense, when the only mistake I ever made in my life was getting involved with—"

She stopped short, her mouth agape in shock at what she had almost said.

Kyle stepped closer. "With me?" he asked softly. He put his hands on her arms.

Mary couldn't tell if Kyle was shaking, or if her own jangling nerves were making her feel so quivery. She knew she shouldn't look up into his eyes, but in the long, tense silence, she couldn't think of anything else. She had to see.

"Was it a mistake, Mary?" Kyle said carefully, softly.

"Definitely," she said. His hands strengthened their hold, and he gently drew her closer. "I thin' warmth in his eyes as his

She got only a glimpse of her a brief tasting of her lips, mouth descended around her and pulled her against him, Kyle wou

she'd been denied for thirteen long years surged dere surface, dancing across her nerve endings and making her feel electric. As their tongues tentatively touched and tasted and then hungrily took their fill, she moaned softly and snaked her hands up to clasp the nape of his neck.

After what seemed like a timeless moment, Kyle began to rub each little vertebra on her spine, then slowly and gently pulled back. Their dazed eyes met and locked, their gazes sated even though their bodies were telling them that the simple kiss had not been enough.

The sound of a printer tapping away somewhere down the hall brought Mary into focus. "Oh, my heavens." She stepped back, freeing herself easily from Kyle's hold.

Lord, what had she done now? She'd come marching into her boss's office full of indignation, and then ... then she'd thrown herself at him. At Kyle Weston, of all people. Never had she behaved so irresponsibly—except once. Horrified by her stupidity, her complete lack of control, she started backing toward the door she strode through so purposefully mere moments before.

"Mary..." Kyle urged, following her.

Mary shook her head frantically and held out a hand to stop him. "No, don't," she groaned. "I'm sorry—I mean, if there's nothing more, I think I'll go on break now."

With that, she turned tail and fled, more confused inside than ever.

Kyle muttered to himself as he gathered his things to go home. He hadn't gotten the answers he'd come to work seeking today. If anything, he was even more puzzled by the diary situation. Today, however, there was another issue clouding his thinking.

He'd kissed her. She'd kiss... as enthusiastic as his own—not ... back. Her response was who was trying to keep her distance. The action of a woman ward had been genuine, he was sure of it. S... rise after to his office to entice him.

The question remained, what was Mary up to? ...me

Leaving the building, Kyle had the distinct impression that he was being watched. Mary? He looked around quickly, then, seeing nothing, shook his head. Maybe he was going completely crackers.

But as he approached his car, he couldn't shake the feeling that someone's eyes were following him. Who could it be? The lot was open and sunny, closed in only on one side by waist-high cement pillars. Face it, he thought, an advertising man wasn't a likely target for a hit. Still . . .

He opened his car door slowly, taking an inordinate amount of time to place his briefcase on the back seat. Then he put on his sunglasses and scoped the area. There was no one in evidence, although he did spot a suspicious cloud of smoke coming from behind a nearby car.

Casually, he shut his door without getting in and sauntered toward the smoke. Coming closer, he spied two sets of legs beneath one of the automobiles—legs encased in very unmenacing sneakers and brightly colored ankle socks. Whoever they were, they were hiding, and he had them cornered between two cars and a concrete pillar. He rounded one of the car's fenders, prepared to scare the hell out of the pranksters, or whatever they were.

What he saw startled him. "Maggie?" he said with an intake of breath.

Maggie slowly came to her feet, as did her companion, a wan redheaded girl who looked more shamed than did Mary's daughter. Maggie stubbed out a cigarette with her tennis shoe and met his gaze with a scowl.

"I was waiting for my mom," she said defiantly.

"Beside a Buick?" Kyle challenged. "Besides, it's nearly six o'clock. You know your mother leaves at five. She's probably worried sick."

"I lost track of time," Maggie replied.

A likely story. There was a silence as Maggie and Kyle regarded each other. What was her game? he wondered, then he frowned. He'd accused Mary of playing games hours ago; maybe he was getting paranoid. Maggie was a crackpot kid. She probably had just been goofing around.

Maggie's friend sidled away from them both. "Uh, I gotta get home, Maggie. It was nice to meet you, Mr. Weston."

"We haven't met," Kyle corrected, "and you're both coming with me."

"What?" the girls cried in unison.

"Where?" Maggie asked.

"I'll take you home."

"But my mother would kill me if—"

"This way," Kyle said, cutting off Maggie's friend. He turned slightly and let them walk ahead of him.

"This is Winona Leary. She's in my class at school," Maggie said as they waited for Kyle to unlock the car doors. Maggie took the front seat.

"It's nice to meet you, Winona," Kyle said. "Does your mother know you hang around parking lots smoking cigarettes?"

"Oh, no, sir!" Winona cried, terror written on her face. "She would just—"

"Winona doesn't smoke," Maggie interjected. "I do." *And just what are you going to do about it?* her tone seemed to imply.

The girl's eyes held a hard, almost accusing glint. Kyle knew that belligerent expression—he'd worn it often in his own adolescence. "I bet you're not afraid of anything," he commented.

"Not much," Maggie agreed.

"What about dying?" Kyle asked.

Maggie shrugged her shoulders as if this argument was nothing new to her. It probably wasn't, Kyle realized. The reason he'd thought of it in the first place was that he remembered his father saying the same thing. That tactic hadn't been too persuasive back then, either.

But on Maggie, his words seemed completely useless. She ran her fingers through her curly brown hair, annoyed, and looked out the window. "The way I figure, everybody dies. James Dean died in a car accident—so did my father, and he was only twenty-eight."

She looked at Kyle then, her eyebrow raised as if she expected him to refute this information.

"Those were accidents," Kyle said. "You're asking for it."

"Do you smoke?"

"I used to," Kyle admitted, although a little lie at that point might have helped his argument.

"Then you really shouldn't preach."

This was a twelve-year-old? Girls when he was twelve had been giggly, silly things, mooning over Robert Redford and listening to the Carpenters.

"On the contrary, I think that makes me more qualified than most. I advise you to quit before you really get hooked."

Maggie shrugged again. They rode the rest of the way to Winona's house in silence, except for Winona's nervous directions from the cramped little back seat. Kyle was struck by the difference between the two friends. Winona was fretful and shy—much easier to deal with, Kyle thought. But Maggie. Maggie looked like her mother, but she had an edge to her, just like those wiry, unmanageable curls her dark hair boasted.

Dark hair? An idea occurred to him. Could Maggie have been the cute brunette Sam Terry had seen from his window? He couldn't imagine that the man couldn't tell a twelve-year-old from a full-grown woman, but then, Sam had said it was night...

"See you, Maggie. Thank you, Mr. Weston," Winona said as she got out of the car. They waited by the curb until she had entered her small house.

The Moore house was only a few blocks away, but Kyle drove them slowly. "So tell me, Maggie," he began, gambling that his hunch was correct, "do you always read people's diaries?"

Maggie's head jerked around, her eyes at first wide with surprise, then narrowing quickly. "How did you know?"

"Just a wild guess," Kyle said.

"Hmm." For once, Maggie seemed unsure of what to say next. "I just thought you'd want to see it," she hazarded, "since it concerns you."

"That's not the point, Maggie. You had no right to read that, much less to show it to me, unless your mother gave you permission."

"You don't think so?" Maggie asked. She appeared to be truly surprised.

"Of course," Kyle said. He turned on his blinker and slowed even more as they approached the turn onto Maggie's block. "Privacy is something a person—"

"I mean," Maggie interrupted, "I thought since you two had, you know...that you might find it *interesting.*"

The girl clearly didn't want a lecture on the Bill of Rights. Kyle knew now how it must feel to walk through a mine field. Maybe he was tackling this all wrong. As he pulled to a stop in front of the old wood frame house Maggie pointed to, he decided to try another angle.

"I know it must seem odd to you that your mother and I...you know." He wasn't able to articulate the bare truth any better than Maggie had.

But Maggie waved his words away and reached for her book bag at her feet. "Oh, I don't care about that," she said, turning to face him. She watched him for a moment, but Kyle was clueless as to how she expected him to respond.

"You adults are so dense sometimes," Maggie said finally. Clutching her backpack to her chest, she narrowed her penetrating stare. But again, Kyle was at a loss to understand the meaning behind the silence that followed.

"Hasn't it occurred to you that you're my *father?*"

With that, she bolted out the door.

Kyle felt a cold chill race through him. Had she said *father?*

He grabbed the door handle and started to get out of the car, until he saw Mary greet Maggie at the front door.

Damn. He wanted to run after Maggie, shake her and ask her some questions. *Father?* But he couldn't very well do that with Mary standing right there. And seeing the questioning look in Mary's eyes as Maggie gestured toward his car, he knew he couldn't explain to Mary what had just happened—even to simply let her know that he'd given Maggie a lift home. He was too confused.

He waved curtly at the two and peeled out onto the narrow street. He caught Mary's curious gaze in the rearview mirror as he turned at the corner.

Immediately, his brain started doing some vital arithmetic. Although events were pretty fuzzy after thirteen years, he did remember that Mary had eloped about two weeks after their one night together. Then Maggie had come along...when?

He didn't know. Sure, he'd heard that Mary had gotten pregnant fast—she had to have, since her husband died not much over two months after their wedding. But had she been pregnant before she married? Perhaps that was the reason she'd decided to take the guy up on his offer in the first place.

The words he'd read in the diary came back to him in a rush. *I think K. W. used something—but what if it didn't work? Time will tell...*

Kyle felt the blood drain from his face. His skin felt clammy and feverish all at once. *Time will tell,* he thought over and over. K.W. Him. A father.

What shocked him most as he drove home was that he'd never thought of this possibility—not even when presented with the evidence. He could have kicked himself. Maybe Mary had been desperate and thought he wouldn't care enough to give two hoots that she was carrying his child. He hadn't discussed the chance of pregnancy with her at the time. He should have comforted her on that score, should have assured her that he cared about what happened to her. He should have . . . but he hadn't.

No, he had treated her like dirt. He'd been so intent on catching that plane, on pursuing his own selfish interests, that he hadn't looked back. Could he truly blame Mary for thinking that he wanted nothing more to do with her—or his child? *His child?* Maggie?

Damnation!

Sam Terry was standing by an elm tree with a gigantic pair of clippers as Kyle approached his drive. He simply couldn't stomach Sam's oh-you-lucky-bachelor banter tonight. In fact, he'd probably slug the guy if he said one word about sowing wild oats. With a muttered oath, Kyle bypassed his block and drove on.

He couldn't go home, he couldn't contact Maggie and he sure as hell couldn't talk to Mary about this. What if none of it was true, anyway? A diary page, a girl's remark—none of it was real evidence of paternity. What he needed was the date of Maggie's birth.

Thirty minutes later Kyle was prying at the Zieglar and Weston personnel file cabinet, the one marked M-Z, with a brass letter opener. Unfortunately, the company appeared to take things like employee confidentiality seriously, because he could find no key to the file cabinet, and it would probably take a hundred sticks of dynamite to blast it open. Wearily, he tossed the letter opener aside.

What was he doing? Yesterday he had read someone's diary, and tonight he was breaking and entering. This path would certainly lead to his moral destruction somewhere down the line.

But what choice did he have? He had to think. Kyle walked to his office, his thoughts centering on Mary and Maggie. Somehow, he had to figure out where he fit into their lives. Or how to make himself fit.

Chapter Four

The cafeteria of Daniel Boone Junior High School, where about one hundred concerned parents were gathered to argue the pros and cons of fried food, seemed like every other school cafeteria that Kyle had ever been in—slightly dingy and aggressively dull in its decor. The air held the unappetizing scent of the day's fish fingers and instant butterscotch pudding. No wonder these parents were so worried about what their kids were eating there, Kyle thought. Just standing in the back of the room was clogging his arteries.

"You can't say fish is bad for kids," a stout lady in the middle of the fray was arguing. "But most kids won't eat it unless it's fried. I know my kids won't."

Several of the people around her bobbed their heads in agreement. Kyle mentally referred to this contingent of the audience as the pro-greasers. At the podium, front and center, Mary was doing her level best to hold out for the anti-grease folk. After ten minutes of watching the proceedings, Kyle had no clue who was winning.

"And what about fried zucchini?" A man heatedly jumped to his feet. "No kid in his right mind's gonna want to eat vegetable medley every day!"

"That's right!" his fellow greasers agreed.

Kyle wanted to clobber them all. Didn't they have more important things to worry about? He had to admit, though, that at first he had been a little interested. After all, he might be sending a kid off to school someday. In fact, he might already have a kid in this very school.

But just the thought of Maggie reminded him of his mission here tonight. Finally, he'd decided that his only recourse was to talk to Mary. Luckily, he'd remembered her Monday night PTA meetings from their dinner at the Brass Kettle.

What exactly he was going to say, however, remained vague in his mind. When the realization that he might actually have a twelve-year-old daughter hit him, in his anger all he'd wanted to do was confront Mary. But confront her with what? Maggie seemed fairly certain that he was her father, but Maggie was a crackpot kid. Obviously, she knew the facts of life—she'd thrown a few of them smack in his face—but he still had no evidence.

He simply had to demand, rationally and reasonably, that Mary tell him the truth. And if Maggie was wrong, and if he ended up making an idiot of himself by mistaking her daughter for his own . . . well, it was a logical error, wasn't it?

"Ky—I mean, Mr. Weston?"

Even though the man seemed to be popping up a lot lately, a PTA meeting was the last place Mary had ever expected to see Kyle Weston. How had he found her, and what had brought him here? Judging by the half-bored, half-stormy expression on his face, it couldn't be anything good.

Then, with the force of a knockout punch, the reason came to her. She'd been anticipating this moment for a long time, and the moment of truth had finally arrived. Kyle Weston had tracked her down, and now he was going to fire her.

She'd practically ordered him to that very afternoon. Not only that, but her own actions had virtually assured that any working relationship between them would be untenable from now on. By any corporate standard, throwing yourself at the boss was rule one of employee no-no's. But that's what she'd done, all right—marched right into the lion's den and hurled herself at him.

And now she had to pay. Desperately, her mind whirred to figure a way out of this mess.

Finally, as if coming out of a daze, Kyle focused in on her and spoke. "Who won?"

"What?" Mary asked, momentarily confused. When he gestured toward the crowd breaking up, she understood. "Oh, you mean the fried foods battle. We're thinking about allowing fried vegetables, but not meat."

Kyle nodded. That sounded reasonable. Now what was he going to say—"By the way, do you happen to know if Maggie's my daughter?" It wasn't a topic you could just casually inject into a conversation.

"Was there something you wanted to see me about, Mr. Weston?"

Kyle let out an exasperated sigh. Little wonder he was having trouble being frank, when Mary insisted on addressing him as if he was the grand pooh-bah. "Please, Mary," he said, "it's just Kyle."

"All right . . . Kyle." Mary drew in a breath, then ventured, "Is this about work?"

"Work?"

Chances were slim, Mary knew, but maybe, just maybe, Kyle had hunted her down to talk shop, not to fire her. "Did something go wrong with the Hadley account?" she asked hopefully.

"Hadley?" He knew he was sounding like a zombie, but Kyle couldn't fathom the woman's thinking. Did she actually think that he'd come all this way on a Monday night to get her ideas on dog food?

But, come to think of it, it wasn't a bad idea—at least, not for openers. From there, he could casually segue onto the topic of Maggie. But not here. The stale cafeteria odor was going to his brain.

"Yes," he said, taking Mary by the arm and steering her toward the doors. "I—I wanted to get your opinion on something. Why don't we meet at the Brass Kettle and discuss it?"

"The Brass Kettle?" Mary eyed him suspiciously. "Couldn't we just talk here?"

"No!" Kyle snapped, then caught himself. He had to stay calm—until he found out for sure this woman had hid a daughter from him for twelve years. Then he could blow.

He smiled. "I'm dying for some coffee, and the restaurant's on our way home, isn't it?"

"Mmm." Kyle took that as a yes, but held his breath as Mary nervously checked her watch. "I guess I could—"

"Great, meet you there in ten minutes."

The longest—and shortest—ten minutes of his life. How on earth was he going to bring the conversation around? *Mmm, good coffee. I know Maggie's my daughter, Mary.* No, that was too blunt. *Mary, is there something I should know about Maggie?* That was better, more open-ended, but still awkward. Kyle sighed as he followed Mary, who seemed to glance in her rearview mirror every ten seconds, looking at him. And no wonder. She probably thought he was a lunatic.

Just be up-front, he told himself. Up-front. He said the word over and over again. If he wanted Mary to be honest, he would have to be truthful, too.

But moments later, as he sat opposite her in a back booth, waiting for the waitress to bring the coffee, truthfulness eluded him. Apparently, it didn't elude Mary.

"I though you wanted to fire me," she said frankly.

"What?" Kyle asked, surprised.

Mary shook her head. "I don't mean to put ideas in your head, but I thought—I mean, after this afternoon..."

"Oh." Somehow, in his furor over Maggie, he'd forgotten about that. The kiss. Instinctively, his gaze zeroed in on Mary's lips. It had been fantastic.

Which made him wonder. Would Mary have kissed him if she was truly trying to hide her daughter from him? Wouldn't she be more cautious than that? Kyle sank a little in the booth.

"It won't happen again, Kyle, I assure you."

Mary's declaration made his ears prick up. He'd instigated the kiss, after all. Maybe she hadn't meant to kiss him back, maybe...

"I—I just wanted you to know that," Mary stammered, rattled by Kyle's unresponsiveness. Why wasn't he saying anything? She was trying to put the matter at rest. To cement the idea, she added, "I'd even be willing to be transferred, if that would make a difference."

"Transferred?" Kyle perked up. What, was she trying to skip the state with his daughter? "Where do you want to go?" he asked suspiciously.

Mary's eyes widened. "I don't know...graphics?"

"Graphics?" Kyle barked. "Where's that?"

Carefully, addressing him as though he was on the verge of lunacy, Mary replied, "That's Ben Sykes's department, Kyle." She looked at him, concerned. "Are you sure you're all right?"

Feeling like a fool, Kyle forced himself to snap to. "Of course," he said.

She glanced doubtfully at him and started to rummage through her handbag. "I think I have an aspirin—"

"I'm not sick, Mary."

She hauled her oversize purse onto the table and began to hunt in earnest. "You don't look well. I'm sure I've got one—"

His hand shot out and covered her wrist. "No, really," he insisted. Her breath caught and her eyes looked into his, then at his hand on her arm. Slowly, she tugged free, shut her purse and returned it to her side.

Twisting her napkin, she laughed nervously. "I guess it's that old mothering instinct rearing its ugly head."

Kyle cleared his throat and sat straighter as the waitress delivered their coffees. "Actually, Mary, that's sort of what I was thinking about. I mean, it's about Maggie..."

He took a slug from his cup and was drawn in by Mary's wide, expectant gaze. Why did he always forget how beautiful her eyes were? Just then, as he stared into those deep blue pools, something she'd said came to him, and he backtracked. "Did you say you wanted to work for Sykes?" He couldn't keep the wounded tone out of his voice.

"Well, if it would make things any better in the office," Mary answered truthfully. It wasn't an easy subject to broach, but maybe it would be better if she was the one to get everything out in the open. Pressing on, she said, "And I want you to know that I understand your...discomfort."

"My discomfort?" Kyle asked, testing her words. Somehow, he didn't think he was in control of this conversation anymore, if he ever had been.

"About what happened between us." Mary sighed. "You know."

"Oh. You mean—"

Mary nodded her head vigorously.

Kyle cleared his throat again. Maybe this was the opening he had been looking for. "Then you agree that what happened between us has had, uh, certain repercussions?"

"I've tried to deny it, I guess," Mary said. "But I can't."

Ha! Now he was getting somewhere.

Mary looked at him anxiously. "I just hope you won't think less of me for it," she continued. "It's rather embarrassing to admit."

Apparently, it was going to be easier to find out the truth about Maggie than he had anticipated. Carefully, tracing the handle on his coffee cup, he coaxed, "Don't feel embarrassed."

"It's just—" Her eyes darted anxiously at him. "It's just I didn't ever think you would come back to Dallas."

Kyle's heart started beating double time. "I didn't think I would, either," he said cautiously. "I guess you were probably surprised when I ran off to California. Right?"

Mary nodded. "Although maybe I shouldn't have been. You'd talked about the West Coast a lot, and how you thought you'd feel freer there."

"But still," Kyle interjected, trying to steer her toward a confession, "you must have been surprised that I left *at that particular time.*"

Her blue eyes veiled their emotion from him. "You didn't even call to say goodbye."

Kyle shifted uncomfortably. "I'm sorry, Mary. I should have."

The slightest of smiles touched her lips, and then she shrugged. "Well, anyway, it's all worked out for the best. Until now, that is."

"What makes now different, especially?"

She shot him an odd glance, as if he was incredibly dense. "We're working together, obviously."

"And that's the only reason you're uncomfortable," he said, giving her an opening.

"Yes," Mary confessed.

Kyle waited, then fidgeted as the pause lengthened. He'd expected her to say, "Yes, other than the fact that I've been hiding your daughter from you for twelve long years." But she didn't. Puzzled, he looked into her eyes. They were staring straight at him without the slightest hint of shiftiness or deceit.

"That's it?" he asked.

"What more do you want me to say?" she asked. "I don't feel that I'm working as efficiently as I should be. And I know that you've been uncomfortable at times, too."

She didn't know *how* uncomfortable, he thought. "I thought there might be something more than that—I mean, beyond efficiency and discomfort."

The way he cast off this ongoing problem pricked at Mary's pride. "Between two professional working adults—especially an executive and a secretary—what could be more disastrous?" she asked.

A child who's been secreted away for over a decade.

Kyle leaned back in the booth and crossed his arms thoughtfully. She didn't sound as if she was lying or hiding something from him. But she had to be, he reasoned. That diary, her quick marriage, Maggie's certainty—all those things pointed to his being the father of her child. But if that was the case, why wasn't Mary more visibly anxious about being around him? Unless, perhaps, after so many years of deceit his paternity was beginning to seem like no big deal to her. The very thought made him seethe.

She was right about one thing, though. He couldn't deny that he'd been distracted lately—now more than ever. Besides, breathing down her neck and waiting for her to slip apparently wasn't going to produce the answers he needed. And this fiasco was proof positive that he wasn't an effective interrogator.

Maybe a little professional distance was just the ticket. Mary might let down her guard a little; also, he'd be able to find an excuse to infiltrate the Moore household. It would be a two-pronged attack, and the best part was that Mary had suggested it herself.

"You're right," he announced.

Mary was stunned. "I am?" Even though he'd been solemnly deliberating across the table from her for agonizing minutes, she couldn't believe that she'd actually swayed his thinking.

"Of course, it's not that I don't enjoy working for you—" she hastened to explain.

Kyle cut her off. "I know, Mary. Actually, I've been thinking about this for some time." He rubbed his chin thoughtfully, more worried by how easily the lie tumbled from his lips than by what he was actually going to say. "In fact, that's what I wanted to talk to you about."

Mary's brows drew up, puzzled. "You just said you wanted to talk about Maggie."

"Ah." Kyle stared at the black liquid in his cup, and the distorted reflection there revealed his panic. He strained to find words to cover his strategic blunder. "Uh, but first I wanted to tell you about this idea I had." He coughed anxiously, feeling a bead of sweat forming on the back of his neck. "And actually," he improvised, "you read my mind."

Mary looked dumbstruck. "I did?" Disbelief turned to suspicion. "About what?"

"I want you to work with Sykes on the Hadley account."

"Me? I mean, you do?"

Kyle nodded. Actually, now that he thought about it, this might be a good way to kill two birds with one stone. "Zieglar didn't buy the happy-dog-is-a-healthy-dog approach, and I can't say I thought much of it myself. We need to come up with an idea pretty quick, and with the California merger, I just don't have the freedom to concentrate on it.''

''But, but—'' Mary fought for a moment to find the diplomatic thing to say. Then, deciding this was a time for bald honesty, she blurted, ''But I'm a secretary!''

''The best,'' Kyle agreed. ''But one thing I found in my own company was that sometimes the best ideas came from people who didn't spend the day tooting their own horns. And I know for a fact that you thought of the Cozy Mattress idea last year.''

''That?'' Mary felt herself blush. ''I just told Ben that if a mattress is really comfortable, you need a good alarm clock.''

''There you go,'' Kyle said. ''Now just ask yourself, 'How do you know if a dog food's really good?' ''

Mary shrugged. ''If it comes with free squeaky toys?'' When Kyle laughed, she added, ''No, I mean it. I'm not an idea person, Kyle. I'm good at helping people, and I've always been happy being a secretary because that's the work I'm good at. Maybe I did help out with the mattress campaign, but if it was all up to me, I'm sure I'd draw a blank.''

Kyle frowned. ''And I'm certain you wouldn't.''

''But surely you would do better—''

''No, I wouldn't.'' His tone took on a more urgent note.

Mary flailed her hands in frustration. ''Kyle, I'm sure you mean well, but—''

''Good, then it's settled.'' Kyle held out his empty cup as the waitress passed the table with the coffeepot.

''Everything okay here, folks?'' she asked.

''Great,'' Kyle said, beaming.

Mary grunted her response, waiting for the woman to leave before she put in, ''Really, it's nice of you to have confidence in me, but I'm afraid I'll disappoint you.''

"You won't," Kyle said, smiling. "Besides, it's not allowed. Now, I think we should talk about this further over dinner."

Mary rolled her eyes over her steaming coffee cup. "The only thing we should be talking about is finding another person to work on Canine Gourmet."

"How about tomorrow night?" Kyle asked, ignoring her comment. "You name the place."

"That's not possible," Mary said flatly.

"Do you like steak?"

Mary slapped her napkin down on the table. "Kyle, listen to me. This isn't going to work." She looked at her watch.

"Okay," Kyle conceded, "why won't it work?"

"For one thing, I don't think putting me on the dog food campaign is wise, and then, we can't go out to eat."

"Why not?"

"Because of Maggie."

Kyle's mental radar perked right up at Mary's excuse. "She can come, too," he said.

"No, she can't," Mary explained, "she's grounded."

"Then I guess your house it is."

Mary felt completely shaken—and not just a little suspicious. Somehow, she felt that Kyle had an ulterior motive at work here. "Dinner would be a disaster."

"I'll cook," Kyle offered. He watched for any sign of Mary's wearing down. If he could get into her house, he knew he could find out the truth about Maggie. He'd get to spend some more time with Mary, too, and that was seeming more appealing by the minute.

"It's not just that, and you know it," Mary said in desperation. "I know that my...behavior this afternoon might have indicated that I think there's still something between us—"

"There is."

"Oh." She blinked in surprise. "But there shouldn't be."

"Why not?" Kyle asked, watching her closely.

"Well..." Mary swallowed hard. Why not? As she stared into those chocolaty brown eyes, the answer didn't come through clearly. A dodge was definitely in order. "Besides, tomorrow's a school night. I have enough trouble getting Maggie to do her homework when there aren't visitors. If you were a parent, you'd understand."

Kyle bristled, then stopped himself. He didn't know the truth. "This will be perfect for her then," he said. "We'll be working, and Maggie will see that even grown-ups have to take work home from time to time."

Mary was speechless. It seemed that Kyle was able to successfully parry any argument she could come up with. The man was sly and dangerous. And now she was out of ways to evade him.

Kyle sensed her acceptance of defeat. "Seven, then?" he asked.

"I suppose so," Mary said, slumping listlessly on the vinyl seat. For her own peace of mind, she added, "This is only business, though."

Kyle pulled out his wallet and threw several dollar bills on the table. "Very serious business," he agreed.

They got up and walked silently to the parking lot. All the while, Kyle battled with himself. It wasn't too late. He could still just ask her point-blank about Maggie. Subterfuge wasn't usually his style.

But then, the whole thing might be a figment of his and Maggie's imaginations. Although that seemed a dim possibility, there was still a chance. Besides, he admitted more selfishly, he wanted to get to know Mary better. He didn't understand it, but somehow her rock solidness appealed to him. Thinking about her sometimes self-effacing humor, he bit back a smile. The lady had more going for her than she was willing to admit.

Just as quickly, his smile turned to a frown. Asking a woman if she'd borne his child wasn't a great get-acquainted line.

"Kyle?"

They had reached the cars. Kyle turned to her, raising an eyebrow in question.

She pulled her keys out of her purse. "You said you wanted to tell me something about Maggie?"

"Oh, uh..." In a split second, Kyle reconsidered, then thought better of it. "Mary, I hate to tell you this, but your daughter's been smoking."

"Grounded for *four more weeks?* What for?"

Mary had decided to hold her tongue about this matter during the car ride from her parents' house, where she often parked Maggie on PTA nights. She didn't believe in doing battle while in traffic, but instead had immediately sat Maggie down in the living room once they got home. She knew she had to be firm, but it was so hard. Did all mothers swing constantly between feeling like a tyrant and a failure?

Taking a breath, she said, "I talked to Kyle Weston tonight, Maggie."

Her daughter's jaw dropped. "Oh." She swallowed. "Did—did he say anything in particular about me?"

Mary sent Maggie a you've-got-to-be-kidding-me look that only two people who know each other inside out can share. "Maggie, he told me flat-out that he'd seen you smoking."

Maggie continued to stare at her, wide-eyed with anticipation. When Mary didn't elaborate, she asked, "That's it?"

Her daughter was beginning to sound like Kyle at the Brass Kettle. Why did it seem that tonight everyone was trying to squeeze more information out of her than she had to give?

"That's it, and in my mind, that's enough." Mary stopped just short of tagging a "young lady" at the end of her sentence. In a more cajoling voice, she added, "Smoking's no joke, Maggie. And don't tell me James Dean did it, either."

"Well, he did."

Mary rolled her eyes. "That was over thirty years ago. No one had warned those poor movie stars not to smoke yet."

"Well—Kyle Weston said he smoked when he was young," Maggie said defensively.

"He did?" Mary thought back. Yes, she did remember seeing him once with a cigarette. In bed. A blush crept up to her hairline.

"What Kyle Weston did or didn't do is none of your concern," she said more heatedly. "You're responsible for your own health."

"Then why should you—"

"Because I'm your mother. Period." Mary took a deep breath. She hated pulling the maternal trump card.

Maggie crossed her arms and sank sulkily down into her chair. "I can't believe Kyle Weston snitched on me. My own—"

Their gazes met—both alert, one anxious and the other quizzical. "What did you say?" Mary asked.

"My own health," Maggie stated hastily, "you said I'm responsible for my own health. Sounds like talk-show baloney to me, but if you say so..."

"Oh." She couldn't believe that Maggie was being so reasonable about this. Usually they argued over any kind of punishment for a grueling half hour, at least. Deciding not to press her luck, Mary cast about for another topic. "Speaking of Kyle Weston, he's coming for dinner tomorrow night."

"He is?"

Mary nodded and warily took note of her daughter's apparent eagerness. "Don't get ideas, Maggie. Just because he snitched—I mean, just because he told me about your smoking doesn't make him a target for revenge."

Maggie nodded exuberantly. "I'll be a perfect angel."

When hell freezes over and there's nowhere left to go, Mary thought suspiciously. "This is only a business dinner," she explained, hoping to firmly quash any nascent matchmaking ideas Maggie might be harboring.

Her daughter bounded out of her chair and crossed to the other side of the living room. "That's great," she said. "If we're having company, I'd better go clean my room."

Clean her room? But who was she to argue? "Good night, then," she said.

Maggie smiled, then ran across the room and pecked Mary on the cheek. "'Night, Mom. Don't worry so much. I promise not to be a pain in the neck forever."

After another quick kiss she was gone. She'd said not to worry, but Mary sat for a good thirty minutes doing just that. Something odd was going on, but she couldn't put her finger on it. She supposed it had to do with Kyle, and her distress over Maggie. In fact, Maggie's sweet behavior tonight was in itself cause for concern.

But perhaps she was being paranoid, she thought. Maybe things were simply going her way.

Chapter Five

Mary flitted nervously from one room to the next making last-minute preparations. She had reiterated to Maggie that this was no big deal, just a friendly business dinner, but inside, she was frantic.

Their modest two-bedroom house seemed even smaller tonight. She couldn't imagine how Kyle would look sitting on the old worn living room love seat, or eating in the dining room, which was probably the size of one of his closets. Perhaps they should have eaten out, Mary thought for a moment. Being in public was safer than having company at home.

But what could happen in her cozy, well-kept house? She was just being panicky—Kyle would probably swagger through her front door loaded with briefcases of work for them to get through. There was no reason to think he was going to try to seduce her or anything like that. And Maggie would be here...

She looked anxiously toward her daughter's closed door. There was another variable that could explode in her face. Maggie had been receptive to the idea of Kyle's coming to dinner—too receptive, now that Mary thought about it. She hoped and prayed that Maggie would behave herself, just this once.

Mostly, though, it was her own behavior that concerned her. Maybe if things had worked out differently, if Kyle had shown a renewed interest in her after Bill had died or after Maggie was born, she would have been able to handle it better. Now she simply felt ill at ease and giddy—emotions very out of place for a thirty-four-year-old mother. Every unoccupied moment she found her thoughts returning to Kyle, dwelling on the past and trying to dredge up every syllable the man had ever spoken to her.

It was wrong. Kyle couldn't like her—not really. What had happened to Cindy Sellars? Why did he want to spend an evening at her humdrum house when he could be having a night on the town with some gorgeous chick? Maybe he saw her as more challenging, or some such nonsense. She doubted it, but that was the only explanation she could think of.

The sound of the doorbell nearly frightened her out of her skin. She looked at her watch. It was seven o'clock on the nose. Taking a deep breath, she again glanced at the three place settings on the dining room table and scanned the living room for anything amiss, then proceeded to the door.

When she opened it, Kyle stood in front of her, freshly groomed and carefully dressed in jeans, an ironed button-down shirt and the leather jacket that Maggie so coveted. Mary found herself admiring the earthy scent of the leather wafting into her little house.

Kyle was loaded down with groceries. No briefcase, Mary noted. "Hope I'm not early," he said, his expression suddenly anxious.

Did she look as though she wasn't ready? She'd changed from her work clothes into a blue knit skirt and blouse hours ago. She wondered if she already appeared rumpled.

"No, you're just on time!" chimed a chipper voice behind her.

When she turned, Mary's jaw nearly dropped to the porch. Maggie, neatly dressed in a denim jumper and a T-shirt, came forward to take some groceries from Kyle. "It was awfully thoughtful of you to bring dinner, Mr. Weston," she said, propping a paper sack on one hip. "Please come in."

Mary was shocked. Usually it took an act of God to get Maggie out of her jeans—even her ballet teacher said so. Now, if it wasn't for a few stray bullet holes in that jumper, she looked almost…sweet. Suspicion followed close on the heels of astonishment. Maggie was no barbarian, but her polite, oozing tone sounded out of character.

"Mom," Maggie mumbled more gruffly in her ear. "You're clogging the doorway."

Suddenly, Mary realized that her own manners were all that was lacking in this case. "Yes," she said, stepping aside, "come in."

"Thanks," Kyle said. "Where's the kitchen?"

"This way," Maggie said, and Kyle followed, leaving Mary to bring up the rear.

During the dinner preparations, Mary found it difficult to break into the spirit of things. Maggie continued to play the tea-party perfect hostess, and Kyle appeared to relish his task of broiling the steaks and whipping up the mashed potatoes. The two of them chattered nonstop about old movies and motorcycles.

Mary kept returning to the emptying grocery bags, searching with dwindling hopes for work-related material. None was in evidence. Her heart did leap expectantly when she hit upon a videotape, but when she took it out of its plastic bag, instead of taped commercials from Zieglar and Weston it turned out to be a copy of *Rebel Without a Cause*.

She held it up. "Uh, Kyle?" When he looked up from the stove, she asked, "This wouldn't possibly have anything to do with Canine Gourmet, would it?"

A smile broke across Kyle's face. "I'd almost forgotten about that. I brought it along as a hostess gift."

"Wow! Cool!" Maggie exclaimed. "Is this really for me—I mean, us?"

"That was very nice of you," Mary said. There went her no-James-Dean rule, she supposed. Kyle smiled again and shrugged charmingly.

Maggie wasted no time in ripping the cellophane off the box and inspecting her first tape of her very own. "Cool," she marveled again.

"Maybe your mom will let us watch it tonight," Kyle said, tearing up lettuce and tossing it in a salad bowl.

Mary started to say something about work, but Maggie immediately put the tape aside. "Oh, no," she said earnestly. "I'm not allowed to watch James Dean movies for another two months."

Kyle shot Mary an apologetic glance. "I'm sorry, I didn't know you were doling out cruel and unusual punishment these days, Mary."

"Actually," Maggie put in before Mary could respond, "according to all the parenting books on Mother's bedroom shelf, she did absolutely the right thing in taking away from me the very thing that I like most in the whole wide world."

"The psychologist who came up with that theory obviously wasn't a fan," Kyle joked.

"*All* the books say that deprivation is an effective tool," Maggie remarked sagely, then she sighed. "And after all, what's a single mother to do, Mr. Weston? In the modern world, it's hard to bring up a kid all by yourself..."

"Okay, okay," Mary said, knowing this was the first step toward a complete cave-in. "This poor single mother will take your grievances under advisement."

Even as he laughed along with the rest, Kyle felt a pang of guilt. Maggie was an operator, all right. She'd made her mom feel guilty and reminded him of his business here all in one fell swoop. He hadn't meant their playful exchange to turn into a two-against-one. In fact, he didn't want to interfere in Mary's child rearing at all. At least, not until he knew he had a right to.

Somehow, he'd just naturally fallen into the banter. Quickly, he stole a glance at Maggie, chopping celery next to him, then at Mary, who was fussing with the water glasses by the sink. Natural...that's what was odd. It seemed strange to him how easily he felt he fit in here, in their kitchen, in their world. Just a week ago, he couldn't have imagined being here, much less actually enjoying himself.

In fact, until Maggie had started laying it on thick with the single-mother business, he'd forgotten why he was here. Mary kept distracting him. It was obvious that she was a little on edge. So was he. Sure, the adrenaline coursing through him had something to do with his uncertainty about Maggie, but the woman standing on the other side of the linoleum floor was contributing more than her fair share, too.

She was being cautious, keeping him at a distance, but her tactic was backfiring. It only made him want to draw her out more—to see one of those rare, radiant smiles of hers directed at him.

"Table's ready," Mary announced from the doorway, interrupting his thoughts. He looked at her. The smile that greeted him was more polite than radiant. Well, he'd work on that during dinner.

"Just in time," he said, slapping the last steak on the platter Mary had provided. "Let's eat."

They situated themselves at the table, with Mary at the head, Kyle to her left and Maggie to her right. Unfolding his napkin, Kyle admitted, "I think this is the first honest to goodness home-cooked meal I've had since I came back from California."

"California?" Across from him, Maggie's eyes were lit with nothing less than awe. "You lived *there?*"

"Until a month ago—" Mary supplied for her daughter, then teased "—didn't you notice his surfer-boy suntan?"

Kyle grinned. "It's fading fast, of course. Sun's such a rare commodity here in Texas."

"That's the truth," Mary shot back. "You have to travel all the way to an open window to get a decent burn in these parts."

"Wow," Maggie said, still stuck on his previous home. "California."

Kyle swallowed and laughed. "It's not *that* exotic, Maggie. They have all the trappings of modern life—congested highways, McDonald's..."

"Movie stars..." Mary added.

Kyle's heart sped at the challenging twinkle in her eye. "Smog."

"San Simeon."

"Malls."

"Malibu."

"It's too cool to be true," Maggie said with a sigh, ignoring the grown-ups' interchange.

Mary shot a knowing glance at Kyle. It didn't take a rocket scientist to figure out what illustrious person her daughter connected to the Golden State.

She was pleased, though, that Maggie had the good manners not to become completely sidetracked by James Dean and instead asked Kyle, "Do you have a mansion there?"

Kyle grimaced as he took a gulp of water. "Uh, I wouldn't call it that. I have a house on the beach."

"And a convertible?" Maggie asked, overwhelmed by the idea of such a glorious place. Before Kyle could answer, she corrected herself. "Oh, but you wouldn't need one. You've got that motorcycle."

"I have a car there, too," Kyle assured her. "In case of blizzards."

Maggie scowled a little at his teasing and turned her attention to her food. As she stabbed a forkful of potatoes, though, her eyes darted back to him for one last question. "Swimming pool?"

"The Pacific Ocean."

Apparently overcome, Maggie let her utensil drop and took a long drink of water.

In this instance, Mary was grateful for Maggie's inquisitiveness. She had never really given serious consideration to Kyle's real life in California. A beach house. The phrase conjured up a mental image of wild parties, bikini-clad beauties...bachelor paradise. That was a stereotype, of course. But on the other hand, he hadn't shrunk from the stereotype when Maggie interrogated him.

Mary frowned as her gaze swept over the quaint suburban floral print on her wallpaper. For all she knew, Kyle could be planning to move back to California once he had made sure the family business in Texas was running smoothly. Not that it would make much difference to her.

"Are, uh, you planning to sell your house?" she asked— very casually—a moment later. Just to keep the conversation going.

Kyle seemed to consider the question carefully. "It's a nice house," he said.

Mary nodded. But what did that mean? "So, I guess you might want to hang on to it. As a vacation home?"

He cocked his head, and his brown eyes studied her for a second. She felt herself blush. Was he attributing some motive to her questions?

"I was just wondering," she added quickly.

Kyle shrugged. "I haven't decided yet."

Which told her nothing. Frustrated, Mary tried to tamp down her curiosity. It was none of her business.

Business.

"I guess what I wanted to know," she said, "was whether you were going to shut down your California office after all."

He leaned back and gave her that unnerving, studying gaze again. Crossing his arms, he said, "You must love advertising."

Mary blinked. "Me? I mean—well, yes, I do..."

"Not many people have your dedication, you know."

She smiled stiffly. Something in the tone of his voice made her leery of what was coming next.

"Usually when employees gather outside the office, they try to delve into one another's personal lives."

Mary's smile felt positively frozen even as a fresh blush crawled up her neck to thaw it out. "I—I had just wondered, since you hadn't said anything about how your business trip this weekend had come out."

"Very satisfactorily." He chuckled, telling her that he wasn't buying her "strictly business" stance. "And for the rest, I'm trying to work out a way to consolidate my company into Zieglar and Weston so I can move here permanently and not have to shut down my old office entirely."

Mary attempted not to dwell too much on the relief she'd felt when he'd said the word "permanently." After all, he was still probably going to be shuttling back and forth, and the business plans could fall through. Either way, he obviously was going to hang onto that house as a getaway—as in, get away from women who got serious ideas about him.

"Well, I'm ready for dessert," Maggie announced, then surprised Mary yet again by jumping up and clearing the table.

"Maggie, Kyle might not be finished," she said as her daughter whisked his plate out from under his nose.

Kyle laughed, but then agreed. "If there's dessert, I'll be glad to have saved some room. What is it?"

"Oh, I had this chocolate cake," Mary said.

Maggie rolled her eyes. "Geez, Mom, you make it sound like it fell from the sky." Leaning closer to Kyle, she explained, "She made it from scratch. My mother is a really great cook, Mr. Weston."

"I'll get the coffee," Mary said, trying to escape. "Would you like some?" she asked Kyle.

"Sure, but I can get it."

Maggie sent him a glare to let him know that this was not acceptable guest behavior. "We'll get it," she said.

In the kitchen, Maggie skidded over to where Mary was working by the coffeepot. "I think he's bored," she said urgently. "Do you think he's bored?"

"Why do you think that?" Mary asked.

"Well, I was. Gosh, Mom, can't you talk about anything besides business? He'll probably never want to come back here again."

Mary walked to the refrigerator to get the milk. "This is a sort of business dinner, Maggie."

Her daughter muttered to herself as she hacked off the slices of cake. Then, as she was trying to balance three dessert plates in two hands, her face lit up. "I know!"

"Maybe you should make a second trip," Mary warned, seeing one of the plates begin to slip in Maggie's fingers.

"I got it," Maggie said, then disappeared.

When Mary rejoined Kyle in the dining room, he was alone with the cake. "Where did Maggie get off to?" Mary wondered.

Kyle shrugged. "She was hot on the trail of something," he said. He took a deep drink of coffee and let the warm liquid work its magic. There was something comforting about sitting in the relaxed privacy of a dining room and simply being with people he enjoyed. He hadn't experienced that in a long time.

"I thought Mr. Weston would like to see our family photo album," Maggie said, walking briskly into the room and slapping the oversize vinyl book on the table.

Kyle's gaze shot from the album to the mischievous look in Maggie's eyes as she dragged the extra chair over and sat next to him.

"Oh, no," Mary said. "Kyle couldn't possibly be interested in those pictures."

"Sure I am," Kyle said quickly. Whatever her motives were, Maggie was right on target as far as he was concerned. Maybe he could find something in that album that would let him know when Maggie was born.

"Really, most of those pictures are awful," Mary insisted, taking a bite of cake.

"Look, Mom, here you are on your *wedding day*." Maggie addressed her mother, but Kyle knew the words were meant for him. "Gee, you look sort of sad."

Kyle looked at Mary. Her brow wrinkled as she peered at the album, which Maggie had practically shoved in his lap by this time. The picture in question was one of her in a white wedding dress, standing in front of a spray of flowers. It was the Mary from his youth beaming back at him, and a wave of memory rushed over him.

"But I'm smiling in that picture," Mary countered, still frowning.

Maggie shook her head slowly. "You may be smiling, but your eyes seem sad to me. Or maybe not sad...unsure. When was this taken?"

"On my wedding day, of course," Mary replied. "January third."

Maggie's eyes darted toward Kyle briefly, and she turned the page. Again, he felt that increasingly familiar stab of guilt. He hated sneaking around Mary like this, but Maggie seemed to be digging out the clues he needed.

"Hmm," Maggie said as she scanned the next pages more intently. "Not many pictures of *my dad* in this book. I thought I'd show Mr. Weston."

Mary looked over. "There's one," she said.

Kyle focused in on a fuzzy Polaroid of a man standing in front of the house he was now sitting in. His guilt quadrupled.

"Still, it's strange that there's only one in this whole big photo album," Maggie said.

"Maggie..." Kyle warned under his breath.

"Bill wasn't a big picture taker," Mary explained, "and of course, he—"

"That's me," Maggie interrupted, indicating a picture of a baby dressed in a cotton jumpsuit, lying on her back.

"When was this taken?" Kyle asked.

"That's Mom with me at the hospital," she continued, ignoring his question and pointing to another one. Her brows knit together dramatically. "Gee, Mom's sad there, too."

Mary dropped her fork and drew closer. "I'm smiling, Maggie! And don't tell me my eyes look sad, either."

Maggie shrugged. "They look that way to me.... Maybe you just photograph weird."

"That was one of the happiest days of my life," Mary insisted.

"Oh, Mother," Maggie moaned, rolling her eyes, "I only meant that you were probably sad because my father wasn't there with you."

PLAY "LUCKY HEARTS" AND GET ...

★ Exciting Silhouette Romance™ novels — FREE

★ Plus a Crystal Pendant Necklace — FREE

THEN CONTINUE YOUR LUCKY STREAK WITH A SWEETHEART OF A DEAL

1. Play Lucky Hearts as instructed on the opposite page.

2. Send back this card and you'll receive brand-new Silhouette Romance™ novels. These books have a cover price of $2.75 each, but they are yours to keep absolutely free.

3. There's no catch. You're under no obligation to buy anything. We charge nothing — ZERO — for your first shipment. And you don't have to make any minimum number of purchases — not even one!

4. The fact is thousands of readers enjoy receiving books by mail from the Silhouette Reader Service. They like the convenience of home delivery...they like getting the best new novels months before they're available in bookstores...and they love our discount prices!

5. We hope that after receiving your free books you'll want to remain a subscriber. But the choice is yours — to continue or cancel, anytime at all! So why not take us up on our invitation, with no risk of any kind. You'll be glad you did!

NOT ACTUAL SIZE

You'll look like a million dollars when you wear this lovely necklace! Its cobra-link chain is a generous 18" long, and the multi-faceted Austrian crystal sparkles like a diamond!

SILHOUETTE'S

With a coin — scratch off the silver card and check below to see how many gifts you get.

YES! I have scratched off the silver card. Please send me all the free gifts for which I qualify. I understand that I am under no obligation to purchase any books, as explained on the back and on the opposite page.

215 CIS AND5
(U-SIL-R-02/94)

NAME

ADDRESS   APT.

CITY   STATE   ZIP

Twenty-one gets you 4 free books, and a free crystal pendant necklace

Twenty gets you 4 free books

Nineteen gets you 3 free books

Eighteen gets you 2 free books

Offer limited to one per household and not valid to current Silhouette Romance™ subscribers. All orders subject to approval.

PRINTED IN U.S.A.

© 1990 HARLEQUIN ENTERPRISES LIMITED.

DETACH AND MAIL CARD TODAY

THE SILHOUETTE READER SERVICE™: HERE'S HOW IT WORKS

Accepting free books places you under no obligation to buy anything. You may keep the books and gift and return the shipping statement marked "cancel". If you do not cancel, about a month later we'll send you 6 additional novels, and bill you just $2.19 each plus 25¢ delivery and applicable sales tax, if any.* That's the complete price—and compared to cover prices of $2.75 each—quite a bargain! You may cancel at anytime, but if you choose to continue, every month we'll send you 6 more books, which you may either purchase at the discount price ... or return at our expense and cancel your subscription.

*Terms and prices subject to change without notice. Sales tax applicable in N.Y.

Kyle positively squirmed. At first he'd been so captured by Mary's smile and sparkling blue eyes that he hadn't really been listening to their argument. But Maggie's last comment got his attention. And then something else did.

Along the side of the picture, in tiny, faint script, was written the date, and then the year. But it was the date he zoomed in on. *September 23.*

He knew his face paled, and he began to feel clammy as he counted. And recounted. Their office party had been two days before Christmas, which meant . . . nine months to the day.

With a snap, Maggie closed the book. "I'm sorry, I guess I did end up boring Mr. Weston."

As she picked up the book and went to the room she had retrieved it from, Kyle held in the urge to snatch it away from her, to get another glimpse of the woman and child. His child, he realized—the chances that she wasn't his were slimmer now than ever.

He glanced at Mary, who was innocently eating her piece of cake again. His own lay untouched on his plate.

"Are you feeling all right?" she asked, concern in her expression.

"Fine," Kyle said, but the word came out as a throaty whisper.

He reached forward and took another sip of coffee, but it didn't give him the warmth it had before. Somehow, he had to pull himself together. He now had the confirmation he'd been seeking, yet instead of the anger he had expected to feel, he was now awash in a sea of very different emotions. Anger was there, of course, equal in magnitude to shame and frustration—and responsibility, that quality he had so lacked when it had counted.

From a doorway behind him, Maggie called out, "I'm going to do my homework now, Mom."

Mary nodded. "All right."

Maggie shut her bedroom door, and they were alone.

"Would you like some more coffee?" Mary asked.

"Sure," Kyle said. "But I hate being waited on."

"It's no problem," Mary insisted. "Why don't you go on into the living room while I get it? I thought we could work there."

Kyle made his way into the comfortable-looking area he had glimpsed coming in. In a daze, he stood in the middle of the room. Something his father used to say came back to him. "Some day you're gonna wake up and find yourself with a family of your own and you won't even know what hit you."

Of course, Kyle, Sr. had also said that about finishing school and getting a real job and falling in love. Kyle had always laughed at his father's theory of becoming a mature adult, which sounded like a hopeless, passive process. Like waiting for a meteor to crash into you.

Well, he wasn't laughing now. He was too busy trying to figure out what hit him.

"Kyle, I hate to say this, but you look like death warmed over."

Mary had put a tray down on the coffee table and was peering anxiously into his face. "You haven't looked right for two days now. If you don't have a doctor here, I can give you the name of ours."

Kyle shook his head. It ached, but somehow he felt he deserved it. And as for Mary, how could she just stand there? They'd had a child together, but that didn't seem to concern her one bit.

"I'm getting you an aspirin right now," Mary insisted, and bustled out of the room.

Wait, he told himself. He still couldn't be sure...even though he was fairly certain. At least he had a fact to back himself up. Nine months to the day. And she had been a virgin, he knew that. Most likely, she hadn't slept with Bill Moore until their wedding night.

"Here, come sit on the couch." Mary led him over to the love seat and they sat down in unison, both of them sinking toward the middle. She scooted farther over to her side before handing him a glass of water and two small tablets, which he gratefully took.

"I think it's stress," she went on as he chased the aspirin down with two swift swallows.

He put down the glass and fixed an ironic stare on her. Stress? She didn't know the half of it.

"I guess you were right about trying to divide up some of your work load," Mary continued saying when he didn't speak. "I still don't think I'm the perfect candidate, but I tried doing some research today..."

And off she went, through descriptions of toilet paper commercials and office product ads, the importance of building name recognition and a virtual dissertation on print versus the electronic media. It wasn't helping his headache, but it gave Kyle some time to think. And something to think about.

Mary had been at Zieglar and Weston for almost fifteen years. One word from him, whether right or wrong, could scare her away from working there, and then where would she and Maggie be?

The fact was, Mary wasn't in love with him, and as attractive as he found her, he couldn't say that he was actually in love with her, either. If Maggie really was his child, what did he expect, that Mary would throw herself in his arms and move into his house the next day? He doubted it. Most likely, she'd go straight to a lawyer.

The important thing was to keep things steady for as long as he could and hope that, when she became more comfortable with him, she would fess up on her own. At least that way, he wouldn't have a door slammed in his face, and he could be sure that Maggie's mother didn't end up in an unemployment line.

"So what do you think?"

Kyle tried to refocus in the silence that followed Mary's question. "I, uh, think you must have done a lot of research today."

Mary exhaled and her shoulders sagged a little. "Well, I've always read the trade magazines circulated around the office, too. But I guess that's not really applied knowledge."

"You're on the right track," Kyle assured her. He leaned back, and so did Mary.

"I guess this is my penance for not letting Maggie have a dog," she moaned.

"Are you more of a cat person?"

"No, I've never really had a pet at all, except a turtle when I was nine, named Herbert. If you needed an ad for turtle food, we'd be in great shape."

He laughed, and Mary smiled. Her blue eyes shone in the lamplight, and her creamy skin almost seemed to glow. He wondered what she had looked like pregnant, if her skin had glowed like this all the time.

Mary shifted. "Coffee's getting cold." The way Kyle was looking at her was making her nervous. Maybe that was just another manifestation of this odd illness he seemed to be suffering from. But then, she had been staring back, and she didn't have sickness as an excuse.

Kyle took a quick sip, then replaced his cup on the tray. "Good coffee," he said.

Mary nodded. After a moment of avoiding eye contact in the silence that followed, she said, "Well, I guess the most important thing is to find a hook."

Kyle looked puzzled. "A hook?" he asked, reaching over to catch a stray wisp of her hair.

"For Canine Gourmet," Mary explained between clenched teeth.

She smelled so good, Kyle thought, scooting imperceptibly closer to her. "I know I'm supposed to be a good adman," he said in a low voice, "but the truth is, dog food is dog food."

Mary shot a glance at him, surprised to discover that he was almost on top of her. How had he done that? But of course, a practiced California playboy probably had no trouble negotiating love seats.

She pressed herself as far over as she could go. "If that was so, how could a dog prefer one brand over another?"

He took her hand in his and turned the palm up. "Personal taste, I guess," he said huskily.

Mary swallowed. "I guess." Her neck was already stiff from tilting away from him.

"I can help that," Kyle said, seeing her stretch. "Let me."

Before Mary knew what was happening, Kyle had her back to his chest and was gently kneading the muscles of her neck and shoulders. At first, the movements of his callused hands made her more tense than before. But slowly, his hands began to work a sort of magic on her. She rolled her chin to her chest.

"That's better," Kyle encouraged huskily.

Tiny prickles seemed to run along the skin of her neck where his breath touched it. Hadn't she forgotten something? Oh, yes. "How would *you* suggest I approach this dog dinner problem?"

Just then, his lips touched her neck, nearly causing Mary to yelp. A swarm of butterflies took up residence in her stomach.

"Well," Kyle said, "just remember, you're selling to people, not animals."

His lips again alighted on her neck, spurring her to speak. "People," she repeated sharply.

"Mmm," Kyle whispered. "People can be mighty fickle characters."

Mary shivered. "How so?"

Kyle placed both hands on her shoulders, and gently nipped at her neck. "Well," he began, working his way up to her earlobe, "sometimes people think they know what's best for themselves." His hands pulled Mary more firmly against his chest. "Then sometimes, it takes someone else to show them that maybe they were wrong...."

Mary sighed. She felt groggy and incredibly alive all at once. "I suppose—" She sucked in her breath when Kyle's tongue traced the shell of her ear. "I suppose that's where I come in," she finished.

Kyle turned her to face him so that she was almost in his lap. "Most definitely," he said, his brown eyes inviting as his mouth descended on hers.

He tasted of coffee and chocolate, and this time his kiss wasn't the least bit tentative. Or maybe she was more sure of herself this time, more sharing. She tilted her head further back, and Kyle immediately took her up on the intuitive invitation.

"Mary," he murmured huskily.

She opened her mouth to respond, but the sound was lost as his tongue entwined with hers. In the back of her mind, she knew they had to stop soon, although for the life of her she couldn't remember why. Maybe it was because of the account, or because he was her boss, or because he had broken her heart...

The doorbell rang, but before Mary could even think of answering it, a door slammed and the sound of footsteps followed.

"Oh, gosh!"

Mary and Kyle sprang apart upon hearing Maggie's voice, but the girl held a palm out and turned her head away as she headed for the door.

"Stay where you are," she insisted. "I'll take care of this."

Mary practically slid off the love seat, her cheeks aflame. From the door, she heard the sound of Mrs. Williamson's voice.

"I'm sorry to be such a bother," the elderly woman said, "but I just realized I'm out of food for Fritz."

"I'll get my coat and walk you to the store," Maggie offered.

Mrs. Williamson came into the entrance hall and peeked into the living room.

"I'll drive Mrs. Williamson," Kyle said from behind Mary.

"Oh..." Mary faltered.

"No!" Maggie exclaimed, throwing on her jean jacket.

"I don't want to be a bother," Mrs. Williamson said.

"It's no bother," Kyle insisted. "I don't want to wear out my welcome."

Mary blushed even more. She'd welcomed him, all right, with open arms. She should be glad he was going. They probably wouldn't have gotten any more work done than they had already—which was zip.

"But—" Maggie began to protest, but apparently stopped to think of something to protest about. Finally, she hit on something. "But I didn't have time to ask you to sponsor me."

"Oh, Maggie," Mary said, "that can wait."

"But it's next week." Maggie's eyes lit up. "In fact, why don't you come, Mr. Weston? It's a walkathon for the hospital next Saturday, and it's outside and you could bring your motorcycle."

Her words had come out in one big rush, but Kyle could get the particulars from Mary later. He knew an opening when he saw one; this would be a perfect chance to see Mary and Maggie again. And sooner than he'd hoped. "I'll be there," he said.

"Oh, but—"

Before Mary could list her reasons for Kyle not to come, he was already ushering Mrs. Williamson out the door. "Good night, Maggie," he said. "I'll see you tomorrow, Mary."

"Bye," Maggie called after him.

Mary and Maggie stood in the doorway and watched Kyle and Mrs. Williamson make their slow way down the walkway. Just before the two were out of earshot, they heard the woman's clear voice ringing in the night.

"My boss at the drugstore sure never took me to any parks."

Chapter Six

In the farthest reaches of the park, out of sight from the designated walking path, Maggie lay on her back under an oak tree. She delved into her pocket for a fresh piece of gum, then popped it into her mouth.

"Time?"

Against the bright afternoon sun, Winona cast a dark anxious shadow against the new grass. "It's almost three, Maggie."

She nodded. "We'll give 'em another half hour or so."

"But..."

Maggie propped herself up on her elbows. "But what?"

"Don't you think your mother's gonna be suspicious when it takes us over three hours just to walk three miles?" Winona's eyebrows drew together nervously.

"We're not doing anything wrong," Maggie pointed out. "Besides, she's probably having too much fun talking to Kyle to notice."

"Mr. Weston scares me," Winona said. "He is good-looking, though."

"I told you so," Maggie gloated, then sent a silent prayer up to the clear blue sky. "It's got to work, it's just got to. Kyle Weston is just too cool to be true."

"But if you said you saw them necking just a couple of days ago..."

Maggie dismissed her friend's observation, although she admitted it was a good sign. "Anything can happen. Besides, my mom can be really dense sometimes."

Winona shrugged. "I don't know...seems like things are going a little too fast. Take it slow—that's what that film in health class said."

"Take it *slow?*" Maggie repeated, aghast. Sometimes Winona could be so dumb she wondered how she could function at all. "Are you crazy? That's what's caused this whole mess. If they take it any slower, I'll be in college before anything good happens."

"Yeah, but in that film—"

"Winona, Mom and Kyle are getting *old*. They don't have time for *Beyond the Birds and the Bees*. Besides, they're obviously beyond all that junk anyway, or else I wouldn't be here."

The thought of going into that nebulous world beyond the strictures featured in *Beyond the Birds and the Bees* brought looks of distaste to both girls' faces. Maggie returned her thoughts to happier things.

"Did you hear me ask Kyle if he was really going to come to the ballet recital?"

"That's a month off yet, Maggie."

"I know. And since he said yes, that means he can't dump Mom again before then. Not that he's going to anyway," she added hastily.

"I still don't know if that was such a good idea..."

Usually, Winona's worry-wart mentality didn't faze Maggie, but where Kyle was concerned, she had to consider every possible pitfall. "Why not?" she asked when her friend didn't elaborate.

"It's just..." Winona bit her lips nervously. "Well, I don't want you to get mad at me for saying this, but the truth is, you're not the greatest dancer, Maggie."

Maggie could feel her face go beet red, and it wasn't because of the sun. Why hadn't she thought of that herself before she'd opened her big mouth and made Kyle promise he would be at the recital? Now she was going to look like a complete dope!

Winona looked at her nervously. "I mean, no offense, 'cause I've skipped as many classes as you have, but we're the stinkiest ones in the class."

"Oh, my gosh." Maggie couldn't believe it. "I really goofed this up."

Her friend nodded. "Most likely, you're hardly gonna be on stage at all. Lisa Dugan is a shoo-in to get the lead part. We're probably going to be stuck in the back row."

"You're right," Maggie moaned. She drew her knees up to her chest and sulked for a good minute. "I hate Lisa Dugan."

"She's cute and blond," Winona agreed sympathetically. "She hasn't missed a class yet."

"You're right. All Kyle's gonna think when he sees that recital is how stupid I look and how cute and talented little Lisa Dugan is."

"You could get sick," Winona suggested.

Maggie considered for a moment. "No, the opportunity's too good."

"Then you're stuck. Mr. Weston's going to come out wishing he'd dumped Lisa Dugan's mother."

"Hmm." Maggie thought and thought and thought. She couldn't uninvite Kyle. As far as she could tell, it was dance or die. "I'm just going to have to learn fast."

"Learn what?" Winona asked.

"Ballet." Maggie stood up and groped into first position. "Is this it?"

Winona frowned and cocked her head sideways. "Your arms are sticking out funny."

Maggie adjusted, then looked at Winona expectantly. "How about now?"

Her friend shook her head. "Maybe," she said, "but don't you think it's kind of a lost cause? I mean, Madame Jarde hates our guts."

"I don't care. Even if I'm in the back row, at least I'll have tried." She frowned as she glanced aside. "It's my elbows. They look crooked or something, don't they?"

Winona nodded. "I think you're going nuts," she said bravely. "You'll never learn all the ballet we've missed in a month. Maybe you'd better smoke a cigarette and think of something else."

"No way," Maggie said. "Little Lisa Dugan doesn't smoke. I'm going to be as perfect as Lisa Dugan in a month or I'm gonna fall on my face trying."

Winona's eyes widened doubtfully, but in the face of Maggie's newfound stoicism, she shrugged. "Okay... but I don't think Mr. Weston will be too impressed if you fall on your face."

Maggie rolled her eyes. "You're a great friend, Winona, a big help. Keep an eye on the time. I'm gonna jeté around for a couple of minutes."

Mary perched on the very edge of the small plaid blanket, craning her neck toward the finish line. Again, Maggie was nowhere in sight. Remembering what happened the last time she'd had neck strain, she forced herself to appear calm.

"Worried?" Kyle asked, seeing right through her belated attempt.

He was stretched out smack in the middle of the blanket like a six-foot cat lazing in sun. There apparently wasn't a tense bone in his body. He wore a long-sleeved knit jersey with the sleeves pushed up to the elbow, and jeans that hugged his lower body the way they usually did only in television commercials. In fact, with the sun glinting on his blond hair, the man *looked* like an ad—probably for some product that promised eternal health, youth and happiness.

He just looked incredibly sexy, which made her all the more nervous. Worried? How could she not be, when her heart flip-flopped every time she looked at him? She'd had a hard enough time at the office dealing with her attraction to Kyle, and now it seemed that Maggie, in her hero worship, was trying to ensure that he popped up during her free time, too. Her daughter was apparently using every activity Mary had forced down her throat as an opportunity to include Kyle in their lives.

That was what worried her, but for Kyle's sake, she merely looked at her watch. "It just seems strange that it's taking them so long." At the finish line, a stout, pale man wiped his forehead as he slowed to a stop.

Kyle smiled. "What can happen to them? They're just walking."

"Crawling seems more like it."

The grin left Kyle's face, and he looked into her eyes. "You worry a lot about Maggie, don't you? I mean, you would have to, as a parent."

The question seemed odd coming from Kyle, but after thinking for a moment, Mary shrugged good-naturedly.

"That's part of my job, I guess. Worrying without being overbearing. It can be a delicate balance sometimes."

Something sparked in his eye. "Maggie can be a handful, can she?"

Mary shook her head. "I never doubt her," she replied. "It's myself I sometimes wonder about."

Kyle plucked a blade of grass, his expression thoughtful. "How so?"

"I don't know how to explain it . . . I suppose it's just an odd thing to wake up one day and discover that *you're* the parent."

Kyle frowned. "I see what you mean."

Encouraged, Mary continued. "Sometimes I hear myself say things to her that I never would have believed I'd ever resort to—things that sitcom moms say that give you the willies."

He nodded. "And stuff like this . . ." He gestured toward the walkathon crowd. "Do the books say you're supposed to encourage your kid to get involved?"

"That's more my own theory," Mary replied. "I didn't want Maggie to become one of those children who were either left alone to watch television all the time, or sent to a day-care center that made them feel like they spent ten hours a day at school. But I'm beginning to question my wisdom on that score."

"I noticed that she complained about the library that night."

Mary laughed. "Complaining is the breath of life to Maggie, but I don't think that's abnormal. What I worry about is her rebellious streak."

Kyle raised a brow comically. "Too much Jimmy Dean?"

Judging from the exasperation that immediately showed itself in her eyes and the way she threw up her hands, Kyle knew he'd hit the bull's-eye.

"I don't understand," Mary said. "*I* never went through a phase like she is—skipping classes, smoking, junior high school activism. But then, I guess I'm a much meeker person by nature. Which makes me wonder whether all this structure in Maggie's life is going to backfire on me."

"And on her."

Mary nodded. "But, fortunately, Maggie has a good head on her shoulders. You might never guess it, but she's mostly an *A* student."

"She reminds me a lot of myself at that age," Kyle said, then laughed. "But I was mostly a *B* student. What's her favorite subject—or let me guess. Science?"

Mary shook her head. "No, dissecting frogs turned her off of that. It's history."

Kyle's eyes widened appreciatively. "That does surprise me."

"She complains about her textbooks being boring, but at the library she dips into the spicier stuff—kings beheading their wives, witches being burned, revolutions." She laughed again. "I think Maggie just likes intrigue."

A shudder went through Kyle. Mary didn't know the half of it. To deflect some of his uneasiness, he pointed out, "Well, that's something she's gotten out of one of your activities."

Mary nibbled her lower lip, which was a nice distraction in itself. She looked especially pretty today in a pair of khaki shorts and a bright red cotton shirt. Her brown hair, which just brushed her shoulders, was loose. It was hard for him to find any difference between Mary now and the woman he'd seen in the wedding picture just a few nights before.

A touch of pink appeared in her cheeks when she caught him gazing at her. She grimaced. "This must seem awfully dull to you. I could talk about Maggie for hours, I guess."

"I wouldn't mind hearing you talk for hours."

Normally the words would have been like a balm. How often in the past decade had she dreamed of having some-one to talk to about Maggie, and the fears she felt about raising a child on her own? She never even felt the need for advice so much as for simply spilling her guts and purging her doubts. Unfortunately, in this case, she was spilling and purging to the wrong person.

She couldn't get over the feeling that Kyle was after something. But what could she have that would bring a confirmed bachelor like Kyle Weston to a walkathon in the park on a Saturday afternoon? When he looked at her like that, she could almost believe that he was simply interested in her. But she held firm to her suspicions.

He appeared to be truly interested in her domestic life, in Maggie. And yet, thirteen years before, the mere mention of the word "marriage" had sent this same man running hell-for-leather to California.

But for all her doubts, she didn't have the nerve to ask him point-blank what his game was. Deep down, it was too seductive to believe that she really was the object of the warm look in those brown eyes, and to accept his compan-ionship at face value. After Bill, she'd never allowed her-self to get involved with another man. Now she was actually considering it—cautiously.

Out of the corner of her eye, she saw an elderly woman crossing the finish line. Walking with a cane, no less. Kyle noticed the woman, too.

"You don't suppose they're lost, do you?"

"I think they might be doing some discreet dawdling," Kyle answered, looking straight at her.

"You mean—?" Mary glanced down at the mere inches of space between them on the blanket and at the two cans of soda that they'd finished forever ago. She knew exactly what he meant. "Oh."

Kyle put his hand over hers and gently brushed the tendons there with his thumb. "What about you?" he asked. "You always talk about Maggie, never yourself."

"What about me?" Mary asked, trying to keep the defensiveness out of her voice.

"Well . . . I know you like to work, and to hang out with Maggie, but is there anything you do just for yourself?"

Mary thought carefully. For herself? She could think of a million things she'd like to do, but her life always seemed so snarled up with others, she never had the time or energy. "I guess," she said, needing to throw something out, "gardening is my hobby. I like to keep flower beds, although I usually poop out before I get down to the nitty-gritty, like trimming the hedges and trees."

Kyle nodded. "That's it?"

Mary laughed. "You're dying to hear me say something really decadent, aren't you? Like that my favorite hobby is taking bubble baths and eating bonbons."

"Sounds good to me," Kyle quipped, although bubble baths really were a step up in his book.

Unexpectedly, even as she laughed along, a pang of sadness shot through Mary. There *was* something she loved, just for its own sake. It wasn't decadent, really, just not something people normally did by themselves. After Bill died, she had stopped, and Maggie had never been that interested.

"What is it?" Kyle's eyes were dark with concern as he looked at her face.

"Orchestras," she said. "I used to love to go to the symphony when I was younger."

Kyle squeezed her hand. "I guess moms aren't supposed to drop everything to catch the latest concerto."

"Sounds stupid, doesn't it?"

"Not at all," Kyle said.

At that moment, two pair of sneakers appeared next to their blanket. Kyle raised his eyes to see Maggie and Winona looking down at them. Both girls had color in their cheeks and were breathing hard.

"Hey," Maggie greeted them. "What have you guys been doing?"

Kyle arched a brow. "Talking about the symphony."

Maggie's face fell. "I hope you're kidding me. For three hours?"

Winona gave her friend a subtle punch in the ribs, but it was too late.

"Three hours?" Mary said. "How could it have taken you three hours?"

Maggie raised her shoulders innocently. "Beats me. Winona and I just got to talking, and the next thing we knew, we were coming in behind the blue-haired crowd." She shrugged again. "Anyway, it wasn't a race."

Behind her, Winona nodded enthusiastically.

"Well, I guess we should go," Mary suggested.

"Why?" Maggie asked. "Uh, it's such a great afternoon, Winona and I could just go sit somewhere if you want us to."

Mary smiled. "You can sit right here—you're making me nervous. And I don't know how you could be winded from walking three miles at a snail's pace."

Maggie and Winona obediently sank to the ground in unison. "We're children of the nineties," Maggie joked. "Too much television."

"And fried food," Kyle added.

Mary stretched back and crossed her legs. "These kids just need more vegetable medley."

The girls groaned their displeasure. "I don't see why we can't just have hamburgers or something simple," Maggie complained. "You'd think we were demanding royal treatment or something."

"Royal treatment," Kyle mused. "Maybe you should. It would be interesting to see what a five-star eight-course dinner would be reduced to when it's mass-produced for cafeterias."

Winona sighed. "The cafeteria food tastes bad no matter what. And it always smells like dog food in there."

Now it was Kyle and Mary's turn to groan. "Let's not talk about dog food," Mary said. "We probably should be going."

"Now?" Maggie said, her tone verging on a whine. "I wanted to ride Kyle's motorcycle." She gestured to the parking lot in the distance, where his bike was parked under a shade tree.

"I don't know, Maggie," Mary said. "Besides, Kyle hasn't offered."

"Oh, please?" Maggie begged. "We wouldn't even have to leave the park."

Kyle looked from Maggie's beckoning blue eyes to Mary's expressionless ones. She was trying not to influence him, he could tell, yet he felt torn. If Mary didn't want Maggie on a motorcycle, he could understand. But still, he loved to give people rides, and Maggie was a game kid.

"We can't do it today," he said finally, remembering a hitch. "I didn't bring an extra helmet."

Maggie opened her mouth to speak, then shut it quickly. She knew better than to make the suggestion that was on the tip of her tongue. Her shoulders sagged despondently.

"Maybe later," Kyle promised, "if Mary doesn't mind."

"I don't mind," Mary said hastily, "as long as you go slow and wear helmets."

"Great!" Maggie cheered. "When?"

Kyle shot a glance at Mary. Defeat was written all over her face, but she was smiling in spite of herself. "How about next Saturday?" Kyle suggested.

"Cool!"

"I was going to offer to help your mom with the yard."

Mary turned a shocked glance on him. "What?"

"The nitty-gritty stuff—I'm strictly a trees and hedge man, myself."

"Oh, no," Mary stammered, "I didn't mean—"

Kyle held out a palm to interrupt her. "Just in thanks for all the work you're doing."

"But I get *paid* for that," Mary insisted.

"All right, then," Kyle said, "because I want to." He couldn't believe he was actually saying that.

"Sounds like a good deal to me," Maggie said, turning to her mother. "You were just saying that we can hardly see out the front windows because of the bushes."

She was beat, and she knew it. "Okay," Mary said. "I'll pencil in shrubs and motorcycles for next Saturday."

Maggie jumped up. "Cool, cool!"

Kyle turned an apologetic glance toward Mary. "Just being neighborly," he lied, to alleviate any debt she might feel trimming hedges incurred on her part.

Her blue eyes seemed to study him carefully. "Thanks," she said finally, smiling.

They got up, folded the blanket and gathered their things. On the way to the parking lot, Kyle and Mary followed silently behind Winona and Maggie. Kyle stopped himself short of taking Mary's hand as they walked.

Deeper and deeper, he thought, worrying briefly about the extent to which he was involving himself in Mary's life. But at the same time, there was satisfaction in it, too. For the first time in as long as he could remember, he felt as if he hadn't frittered away a Saturday, doing mindless stuff just for the heck of it because he had nothing better going.

Today, he felt he'd actually made some progress in getting to know Mary. Eventually, when she got to know and trust him, he was sure she would tell him about Maggie. And in the meantime, thanks partially to Maggie herself, he had next Saturday to look forward to.

* * *

"*Allo,* Mrs. Moore?" the grating voice on the phone announced, "this is Madame Jarde!"

"Uh, yes," Mary said meekly, "what can I do for you? I hope Maggie hasn't done anything wrong." Although strangely, Mary felt as if *she* was the one who had.

But to her surprise, Madame Jarde answered warmly, "Not at all. Yesterday in class, Maggie was exemplary."

"Oh." Mary didn't know what to say. "I guess I'm glad to hear that."

"*Très bien.* I thought this you should know."

"Well, yes, thank you."

"*Au revoir!*"

Slowly, Mary gently placed the receiver on its cradle, as if sudden movements would bring the frightening Frenchwoman back. With the usual bad news...

Before her hand had lifted all the way, someone banged on the door of the small office she'd been removed to just yesterday. Startled, Mary looked up, half expecting to see Madame Jarde herself looming in her doorway. Instead, there was a man in a suit standing behind a huge bouquet. For a moment, the person's head was obscured by a dazzling spray of roses and eucalyptus leaves, then Ben Sykes peered around at her.

"Surprise!" he said, coming in. "I found these for you at the front desk."

Mary got out of her swivel chair as he placed the bouquet on her file cabinet.

"And if they don't surprise you," Ben went on as she opened the attached card, "they're guaranteed to open your sinuses."

Mary laughed, then frowned. Inside the envelope were two tickets to the symphony for Saturday. The card itself read only, Care to share?

Ben looked on curiously. "Secret admirer?"

She nodded. "Guess so."

"Strauss," Ben said, glancing at the tickets. "And orchestra seats, too. Your secret admirer has class."

"He's got a nerve, that's for sure," Mary said, wishing Kyle at least hadn't sent the flowers to the office.

Ben laughed. "I should have sent you flowers myself. Did you see how happy Zieglar was with your ideas for Canine Gourmet?"

"He did seem to like them, didn't he?"

"This morning was the first time I've seen the man crack a smile in five years." He gave her an exaggerated bow. "Mary, from this moment on, I'm your very open admirer. I don't know how you did it, just keep it up."

"Or you'll stop admiring me?"

"Worse," he agreed, "you'll be doing chiropractor copy for the Sunday TV magazine."

After Ben left, Mary sank into her chair again. She looked at the telephone, then at the flowers, then at the door. First she'd received a glowing—comparatively—report from Maggie's ballet teacher, then these flowers, then praise from Ben.

Something was wrong. Everything was simply too...rosy.

The soothing smell of the flowers and leaves soon filled the little room. On the other hand, why shouldn't she just blindly accept her good fortune? Possibly, just possibly, Maggie had turned a corner and was about to leave her adolescent woes behind. Kyle could truly be interested in her; the symphony tickets were certainly thoughtful. And work, well, maybe she was getting the hang of it, after all.

In satisfaction, she propped her feet up on one of her file cabinet drawers and sighed. At this precise moment, life seemed about as good as it came.

Which made her suspicious. Life wasn't this good until...Kyle. It was Kyle who created that giddy little feeling in her stomach, and Kyle who arranged for her to work under Ben. And as much as she hated to acknowledge it, she suspected Kyle had something to do with Maggie's recent turnaround. The timing was just too coincidental.

She chewed her lower lip anxiously. Never in the last thirteen years would she have expected her happiness to be in Kyle's hands—and she certainly didn't want it to be in them now. When she was twenty, she'd thought he was the answer to her prayers. But when he'd left, and especially after Bill had died, she'd realized the truth. People had to find their own answers, not depend on other people to create happiness. Even if it meant living, working and struggling alone.

Her practical side, which was really almost both sides, told her to proceed with caution. Flowers and concert tickets didn't add up to stability and happiness. They were a quick fix—just up Kyle's alley. And in her book, Kyle didn't have a very strong track record in the area of dependability.

Overwhelming all that, though, was that one tiny, long-ignored part of her that reveled in the excitement and anticipation. Quick fix? So what! She was a big girl now; if disappointment came, she could handle it. In the meantime, life was too short to stand on the edges and keep people at a distance.

Picking up the phone again, she punched in Kyle's extension.

Chapter Seven

Treat your dog like royalty.

Mary looked at the phrase written on her legal pad, accompanied by an entire page of elaborate doodling, and put her pen aside. The slogan sounded about as catchy as "a healthy dog is a happy dog." Something was missing.

The sound of a motorcycle puttering slowly down her street did nothing for her concentration, either. She peeked through a now permanent chink in the blinds. Since the hedge in front of the window had been trimmed, she could see Kyle and Maggie perfectly, both looking like aliens in their round plastic helmets, circling the block for the umpteenth time.

Vroom, vroom, vroom!

Maggie had been in hog heaven when, after she and Kyle had finished in the yard and he'd given her a short lesson in safety, they roared off for a spin. A couple of spins, Mary corrected herself. The whine of that machine was probably driving her neighbors crazy—she knew it was driving *her* crazy. But she was glad Kyle was apparently restraining himself from showing

Maggie the fine art of hot-rodding, keeping the speed down to Mary's suggested ten miles an hour.

But the bike was letting off a sickly, strained whir, as if it was just itching to jump into the next gear. Perhaps it wouldn't be so distracting if Kyle speeded up a little.

Vroom, vroom, vroom!

Mary tensed and stared through the blinds again. There they went, both laughing and hollering to each other above the motor's roar.

Maybe it was good that Maggie was finally getting an outlet for her nascent hoodlum instincts, Mary thought with a smile. She couldn't deny that Kyle's presence perked Maggie up. Mary had long worried about the lack of an adult male figure in Maggie's life. Now it seemed that one had dropped out of the sky, tailor-made for her daughter. And for her.

"Mary?" Mrs. Williamson called from behind the screen door.

"Hello," Mary said. She could just imagine what had brought her neighbor over. "Is there something I can do for you?"

"Is that *Maggie* I've been seeing with that strange man on the motorcycle?" She gestured toward the street, which was empty at the moment. But Mary knew it was just a matter of minutes before her two daredevils came puttering around the corner.

"I'm afraid so," she admitted.

Mrs. Williamson's mouth dropped open. "Why, Mary! I thought you had more sense than that."

"Oh, but—"

"Why, those vehicles are dangerous. And that person driving her around doesn't look like a middle school student to me."

Vroom, vroom, vroom!

"That's Kyle, Mrs. Williamson."

"Kyle Weston?" The lady swung around to inspect him. Quite a few others were out on their porches taking a look, too. "You're right, it's him."

Mrs. Williamson turned back around with a positively beatific smile on her face. "Isn't that sweet of him to give Maggie a ride?"

"Yes, it is," Mary said, amazed by the woman's change of heart. But she'd suspected Mrs. Williamson held a soft spot for him since she'd learned that it was he who had suggested getting her hearing aid fixed. And fetching food for Fritz that evening hadn't hurt his reputation any, either.

"Hey, Mom!" Maggie cried. She and Kyle were idling at the curb.

Mrs. Williamson, in a surprising show of spryness, scurried down the sidewalk to them. Mary followed.

"Want a ride?" Kyle asked the elderly lady with a mischievous grin.

"Me?" Mrs. Williamson chuckled. "That thing's too fast for even me, I'm afraid. I was just about to walk down to the store for some food for Fritz."

"We'll get it, won't we, Kyle?" Maggie asked, obviously eager for an excuse to stay on that bike. Kyle had finally insisted that she stop calling him Mr. Weston, which for her had apparently sealed their bond of camaraderie.

"Sure thing," Kyle said. "What kind do you need?"

"Canine Gourmet," Mrs. Williamson replied. "What other kind is there?"

Kyle and Mary shot each other pointed glances. "That's what I'm beginning to wonder," Kyle said. "You on tight, Maggie?"

"All ready," Maggie replied, bracing herself.

In an instant they were off, crawling down the street.

Mrs. Williamson sighed as she watched him leave. "He's such a nice man."

Mary was still frozen in disbelief. Here was her next door neighbor, a bona fide Canine Gourmet customer. The opportunity was too good to pass up.

"Do you really buy Canine Gourmet?" she asked.

"Of course!" Mrs. Williamson said. "Fritz deserves the very best." She looked back to Kyle and Maggie as they disappeared around the corner. "He's so handsome."

"Fritz?" Mary asked, her mind still on dog food.

Mrs. Williamson stared at her in amazement. "Mr. Weston," she clarified.

"Oh." Mary cleared her throat. "I was just wondering about Fritz. Why do you buy Canine Gourmet, Mrs. Williamson?" She felt like an idiot, giving her neighbor the third degree like this. Like one of those people on television commercials who stuck microphones in people's faces and ask them why they bought a particular brand of toilet paper or coffee.

"Well," Mrs. Williamson began thoughtfully. *She* looked like one of those people on commercials, too. "I've heard it's the most nutritious kind. And a healthy dog is a happy dog, you know."

Mary's hopes for this experiment sagged. That was the last thing she'd wanted to hear.

Mrs. Williamson put her hands on her hips. "Mary Moore, are you thinking about getting a dog?"

"Me?" Mary asked. "No, I was just a little curious about... what Fritz liked to eat." Giving it one more try, she asked, "Is there any particular feeling you derive from feeding him Canine Gourmet?"

To her surprise, Mrs. Williamson seemed truly grabbed by the question. She pondered for a moment. "Well, I feel good, I know that."

"Uh-huh," Mary coaxed. "Why's that?"

"I don't know. I suppose it's because of the crystal bowl I put Fritz's food in."

Mary regarded her neighbor skeptically. *"Crystal?"*

"Fritz is practically all I have. The least I can do is give him the red-carpet treatment twice a day."

Mary crossed her arms and chewed on her lower lip, thinking it over.

"Was that the right answer?" Mrs. Williamson asked hesitantly.

"Precisely right," Mary replied.

Coming out of the grocery store, Kyle handed Maggie the bag with the dog food. "You can be the bag *meister*."

Maggie laughed as she hopped behind him on the bike. "This has been the best day, Kyle. It's just been too cool to be true."

Kyle started the bike and headed off down the street, a grin plastered all over his face for the world to see. Maggie wasn't the only person who felt that way.

It had been touch and go to begin with. This morning he realized that he didn't have the keys to his father's tool shed. Having shunned yard work like the plague, he'd never even asked his father's maid, who still came in to clean twice a week, where those keys were. With no tools, he could hardly expect to wow Mary with his tree-trimming skill.

So he'd been forced to swallow his pride and go begging next door.

"Oh, bud," Sam Terry had murmured ominously, "this sounds bad. You so bored that you're gonna finally trim those holly bushes?"

"Actually," Kyle had admitted, "I'm doing it for a friend."

Sam's eyes had widened, and then he'd chortled. "I haven't known you long, bud, but I never thought I'd see this day."

"It's no biggie," Kyle had replied, annoyed, wishing the man would stop gloating and hand over the damned clippers. "I'm just doing it this once."

Sam winked sagely. "Yeah, I said that myself once upon a time. They always get you in the end, bud. From there on out, it's happily-ever-after, hedges and hardware store bills. Those clippers will as soon trim your wings as a bush, mark my words.''

''I'll consider myself warned.''

He'd muddled through the yard work somehow, even though he didn't really know a rose bush from a rhododendron. Still didn't, but he'd hacked Mary's yard into some kind of shape, at least. And far from feeling put upon, as Sam had warned, he felt satisfied, almost smug—as though he had done something manlike that bonded him to Mary and Maggie somehow.

As if to point out the tenuousness of that bond, Maggie shouted in his ear. ''Ready for your big date tonight?''

Kyle laughed. ''I might need a shower...''

He couldn't tell, but he imagined Maggie rolling her big blue eyes that were so like Mary's. ''You know what I mean.''

''Yeah,'' he assured her. ''I'm ready.''

The understatement and overstatement of the century. What he felt ready for was taking Mary in his arms and kissing her until they were both worn out. What he wasn't ready for was telling the truth, but it had to be done.

He hadn't been prepared for the overwhelming guilt he would feel about all this. At first he'd been so angry with Mary for keeping the truth from him that he hadn't felt any compunction about being in collusion with her daughter. But now, every time Maggie gave him a sly glance or when Mary looked up at him with those trusting blue eyes, something stabbed at him. Sooner or later, he was going to have to tell Mary that he had read her diary—and the sooner the better.

Every time he saw her, he was painting himself into a narrower and narrower corner. Once he confessed, his only defense would be an offensive one—that if she hadn't hidden Maggie away for so long, they could have gotten this all out in the open long ago. After that, it was anybody's guess how she would respond.

In his mind, he pictured taking her in his arms, explaining how torn apart inside he'd felt when he'd discovered Maggie was his daughter. He would assure her that things were different now, that he was in her life to stay, if she wanted him there. . . .

God, he prayed that she wanted him there.

"I hope you don't blow it."

The words could have been his own, but they'd come from Maggie. He smiled. Maggie was an operator, all right, but he knew where she was coming from. Having just lost his own father, he understood her need to secure one for herself. And, as odd as it seemed, stepping into the role didn't feel as uncomfortable as he'd first thought it would. But the extent to which he would be able to also hinged on Mary.

"Me, too," he replied as they approached Mary's house.

She and Mrs. Williamson were still standing where they had left them. "That was fast," Mary said as they came to a stop.

"Kyle has to go home," Maggie stated flatly as she got off the bike.

"I do?" Kyle asked.

"I made some iced tea," Mary offered.

"It's getting late, Mom," Maggie said. "You're supposed to call Grandpa to tell him when to pick me up."

Kyle caught the martyred tone in Maggie's voice at the idea of being shipped off to the grandparents during their date; it was obviously her sacrifice for the cause. "I'm sorry if we're putting you out, Maggie."

"That's all right," Maggie replied graciously, "I like to *spend the night* with my grandparents."

Kyle's heart tripped a beat. The message was received loud and clear. By the way Mary was shuffling the tips of her sneakers in the grass, Kyle could tell she was a little uncomfortable having this information out in the open before the date had even begun. Not him. It would give him something to think about—and time to arm himself for the best-case scenario.

"Well, I guess I should be going," he said finally.

"Oh, wait," Mrs. Williamson said. She offered him some money for the dog food and thanked him. "I hope to see you again soon," she added.

Mary waved as he started up his bike. "See you tonight," she said.

"Till tonight," Kyle replied.

Behind Mary, Maggie mouthed the words "Don't blow it" once again, then turned and scampered up to the porch ahead of Mary.

Mary collapsed on the bed, her panty hose at her knees. She felt hot and dizzy, much as she had all day—ever since Maggie had not so subtly pointed out for Kyle that they would have the house to themselves tonight. Was she a moron? Why had she even given herself that opening? Maybe when her father arrived for Maggie, she would tell him she'd be picking Maggie up later. Or maybe...

Or maybe she should just exercise a little willpower. She wasn't a teenager anymore. But this was Kyle, she reminded herself. Thirteen years had done nothing to dull her attraction, or susceptibility, to the man.

On the other hand, it was entirely possible that he was only interested in the symphony. But even as the thought occurred to her, she dismissed it. The glint in his eye immediately after Maggie's pronouncement spoke for itself.

"Mom!"

Maggie raced into the room and stood nervously over the bed. "Aren't you feeling well? Can I get you anything?"

Maggie's concerned, solicitous voice as she loomed over her brought Mary upright quicker than would have been the case if Kyle himself had appeared. She immediately began to pull up her panty hose and set her hair to rights, which had been mussed when she flopped backward on the bed.

"You don't look good at all!" Maggie exclaimed.

"Thanks, Maggie." She got up and walked to her dresser.

"Is *this* what you're gonna wear?" Maggie held up the navy blue dress that Mary had laid out, holding it up to herself. The dress engulfed her gangly, twelve-year-old frame.

"Oh, Mom." Maggie's tone was so full of dread that Mary looked up from the mirror.

"What's the matter with it?"

"It's so—" Maggie frowned. "Well, it's sort of dumpy, don't you think?"

Had she not been nervous, Mary would have laughed at the spectacle of her daughter, whose taste in fashion didn't go beyond oversize sweatshirts, passing judgment on her best silk dress. Maggie was obviously concerned about the high neck, but Mary had chosen it for that reason. If she couldn't hold her hormones in check, maybe her clothes would.

"Don't you have anything red?" Maggie asked. "With sequins, maybe?"

"Maggie! Do you want me to go to the symphony looking like a—"

"I know what a prostitute is," Maggie said when Mary didn't finish her sentence. "I just thought you might want something flashier, is all."

After finishing with her makeup, Mary slipped the dress over her head. Maggie zipped up the back.

"Hmm," her daughter said, surveying the result. "It looks okay on. And you fill it out better than I thought you would."

Before Mary could say anything to that remark, the doorbell rang.

"I'll get it!" Maggie tore out of the room, shouting as if Mary was blocks away instead of mere feet.

From the voices traveling into her room, she knew that both men had arrived at once. Now was her chance, she thought. With a word to her father, she could save herself and let Kyle know that this was not going to be a date of the hot and steamy variety.

She stepped into her heels and gave herself one last quick inspection. Then she went out to greet the night.

The three of them were talking in low voices in the living room. Her father, a tall, stoop-shouldered man with a circle of tufty gray hair around his bald head, beamed when he saw her.

"Plotting against me?" she asked.

"You look beautiful, Mary," her father said.

In the background, Kyle murmured his assent, but the appreciation that sparked in his eyes spoke louder. He stepped forward and presented her with a small bouquet of roses.

"Thank you." She breathed in the sharp fragrance, then looked up into his eyes. The desire she saw in those brown pools did nothing to quell the butterflies in her stomach. And yet she couldn't bring herself to pull her gaze away until Maggie spoke.

"Bye, Mom," her daughter said. "Bye, Kyle."

Mary turned just as her father's back was disappearing through the doorway. Suddenly, she remembered that she had meant to say something. She ran forward quickly.

"Wait!"

Kyle came up behind her and touched his hands to her elbows as her father turned. The feel of Kyle's hands sent little shock waves up her arms. She could feel his breath, gentle on the back of her neck.

She lifted a hand that felt as heavy as lead and waved after Maggie and her father. "I'll see you tomorrow," she called, and didn't dare look back.

"So what do you think?" Kyle asked during the brief intermission.

"I love waltzes," Mary said. "They always make me feel like I'm living in a dream world of palaces and privilege."

Kyle smiled. "Instead of PTA meetings and TV ads?" he asked wryly.

Mary laughed. "I guess it sounds pretty stupid."

He shook his head. "Not at all. If we didn't have music and the other arts to take us out of our lives sometimes, I think we'd all go crazy."

In his dark gray suit and white shirt, Kyle looked as handsome as sin. Mary frowned. "I've never liked the idea of escaping reality," she said. "Daydreaming tends to distract people from finding practical solutions to their problems."

"Well," Kyle assured her with levity, "we won't be escaping for too much longer. The last half of the concert doesn't look too long. Then you can release your palace guards until the next symphony."

Mary returned his laugh, but the exchange put her on guard. Thirteen years notwithstanding, he was still a quick-fix man, and she was as practical as ever. Oh, that dreamy side of her still reared its head—if not as violently as it did long ago when she had fallen in love with the boss's son. But she could control it now.

Couldn't she?

All during their intimate dinner and the first half of the program, she couldn't quell that weightless, giddy feeling that seeing the admiration in Kyle's eyes gave her. Every time he touched her to help her into a chair or lead her through a door, her heart galloped way ahead of her reason. Was it so wrong to enjoy being in the company of such an attractive man? Or was it just the fact that it was this particular man that made her so uneasy?

The music following intermission was just as beautiful as in the first half, and again Mary was swept away. Sometime during "The Emperor Waltz," Kyle's hand captured hers, and continued to hold her hand after the concert ended and they were walking to the car.

When they were both buckled into the front seat of Kyle's sports car, he turned to her. One blond brow darted upward in question. "Home?" he asked.

Mary nodded. "Guess so." It was late, and she really wasn't one to go for a drink.

But her decision left her only fifteen minutes or so to contemplate how she was going to handle the rest of the evening. As they sped down the night-lit streets, she considered the possibilities. Her nerves jangled as if stimulated by a drug, and with a jolt, she realized what the sensation really represented. Desire.

Pure and simple. She wanted Kyle—wanted him to stay the night with her. As fraught with possibly disastrous consequences as this feeling was, she couldn't deny it.

But could she actually give in to it, either? As the miles ticked by, her panic escalated. By far the most practical solution was to hop out of the car as fast as humanly possible once they'd reached her door.

When that moment arrived, however, she choked. Kyle killed the engine, and in the darkness, turned to her expectantly. Was he going to kiss her here, in the car, like two kids necking after a Saturday night date?

The twisting sensation in her stomach spurred her to action. "Would you like to come in?" she asked hastily.

She could see his white teeth in the moonlight. "I'd love to," he said.

As Mary mumbled about making a quick pot of coffee, Kyle followed her up the sidewalk. God, he wanted her. All night long he'd been tortured looking into those beautiful blue eyes, smelling her perfume, touching her... and knowing that they had the prospect of two empty houses and a long uninterrupted night dangling enticingly in front of them.

For all his wanting, though, he had been surprised that she'd actually invited him in. Doing so showed no small measure of trust on her part.

Trust. The word gnawed angrily at him. As much as he wanted her, he couldn't stay the night in her house without coming clean first. He had to tell her what he knew or he'd never earn her complete trust or respect.

Mary closed the door behind them. In the dim light of her entrance hall, she turned to him.

Her blue eyes were dark as they looked into his. "Coffee?" she asked.

Coffee was the last thing on his mind. Words, even the ones that he'd been practicing since he'd first discovered Maggie was his daughter, eluded him. And the only action that seemed natural at that moment was to step forward and take Mary in his arms.

To his surprise, Mary stepped forward, too, and wrapped her arms around him without the slightest hint of shyness. He'd intended for the kiss to be gentle, but soon his long held back need took over. He'd anticipated this moment all week, and now, moving his tongue along the ridge of her teeth, he wondered if he had thought about anything else for the past thirteen years.

Their bodies fit together perfectly, as though they were made for the express purpose of finding each other. It was impossible not to pull Mary closer, just as it seemed impossible that she wouldn't cleave to him in return. He felt himself responding to her softness, the rhythm of her tongue, the movement of her hands along his shoulders and back.

Quickly, his will to take it slowly was relenting. But still, a voice in the back of his mind kept up a constant reminder. *Trust*, it said. *It's not too late.*

He dragged his mouth away from hers and buried his face in her hair, breathing in its clean scent. Clean. He had to come clean.

His breathing was ragged and every inch of him was screaming with need, and he could feel Mary's body stiffen, too, when he ended the kiss. Tentatively, she looked up at him.

"Kyle?" she asked, then set her mouth determinedly. "I don't mind."

"Oh, Mary," he groaned.

Mary looked into Kyle's tense features, confused. "Kyle, what's wrong?"

He brought his hands to rest on her shoulders, putting some distance between their bodies. "I want you, Mary, make no mistake."

"Kyle, I—I don't want you to pretend to be in love with me. It's not necessary."

Kyle could feel his face fall. With those words, he realized anew how much he'd hurt her before and how much he'd hoped to make it up to her now.

"Mary, you're wrong if you think I don't care." The past week, the happy days they'd spent together, all his newfound pleasure came rushing back to him. He pulled her to him and gave her a tight squeeze. "I'm so crazy for you I'm numb."

Mary laughed and hugged him close in return. "What did you say?"

He looked at her and smiled. The desire, relief and utter joy he saw in her eyes, and in his own, which were reflected in hers, overwhelmed him. "I said I'm so besotted I'm numb."

Their gazes remained locked, but in a second, everything changed. The shock of realization that tore through his body made him stiffen. In a flash, the desire in Mary's eyes turned to doubt, the joy to a seminal spark of betrayal.

"What did you say?" she asked again, this time in a low, tense voice. But Kyle knew that she remembered.

"Mary, I—" His mind fumbled and then failed to find words to explain himself. Suddenly, there seemed no way to justify what he'd done to her. Not thirteen years ago, and not in the past weeks.

"I don't understand," Mary said in confusion. He'd said the very words she'd written in her diary, but how would he have known that? She looked at him steadily, trying to come up with an answer. "What have you done?"

Kyle took a deep breath. "Mary, I didn't mean to hurt you."

The words sent a flush of red into her cheeks. "Hurt me?" she asked. "Kyle, just tell me. What did you do?"

"I read your diary, Mary. Maggie showed it to me."

If he'd slapped her, she couldn't have looked any more shocked and stung than she did at that moment. "Maggie?" she asked, stunned.

In a flash, Mary remembered all the things—personal, deeply emotional words—she'd written in her spiral notebook. Maggie had shown all that to him? But why?

"It's not her fault," Kyle hastened to explain. He wanted to take her in his arms again, but he could tell she wouldn't abide that. But standing there, with her staring at him with that betrayed expression, made his tongue feel thick and his words awkward. "I mean, she showed me some pages from your old diary because—because she thinks I'm her father."

Mary listened to his words carefully, but they seemed so farfetched it was if he was speaking in code. *"Father?"* she asked.

"Because she figured out how we were involved before, so close to your marriage."

"What!" The word came out as almost a shriek. She balled her fists at her sides and closed her eyes in an attempt to compose herself. "Kyle, please," she grated out, "please tell me you set her straight."

Streaks of red appeared in his neck. "Mary, I'm sorry." He swallowed. "I'm still not sure of the truth myself."

Suddenly, it all made sense to her. His giving Maggie a ride home and then popping up at the PTA meeting, his looking into her photo album and the questions about her daughter, his calculated seduction of her tonight. Kyle Weston, after thirteen long years, thought he had a daughter. And now he was here to claim her, by hook or by crook.

"Get out of my house."

Kyle's eyes widened at the venom in her tone. "Mary, you don't—"

"Get out," she repeated. When he continued to stand, rooted in place, she let loose her anger. "I can't believe you have the nerve! After thirteen years, Kyle. Thirteen years! Why didn't you just ask me—why didn't you just ask me all those years ago, when it would have made sense to?"

"Then Maggie—" Kyle faltered, and Mary had to take a deep breath to hold down the scream she felt lodged in her throat.

"No, Kyle," she said. "Maggie's not your daughter." That she would even have to deny such a thing galled her. She took two steps to the door and put her hand on the knob. She wanted to be alone.

"Mary, I'm sorry."

"Sorry?" she asked. "Who are you sorry for? Yourself, because you've never had a meaningful enough relationship to have children?"

The words stung, but Kyle shook his head. "I'm sorry that I've hurt you, Mary. I *will* make it up to you."

"You can't make it up, Kyle, not this time." Mary's eyes had lost some of their spark; he detected regret in them now. "And the person you should really be sorry for is Maggie. I still can't believe you would have misled her like this."

"I didn't mean to."

"Couldn't you see how impressionable she was? She was chomping at the bit to find a hero, Kyle. Now what am I supposed to tell her?"

Kyle shook his head. "If you want, I'll talk to her."

"No," Mary said flatly. "I'll work it out with her myself. Right now, it would be best if you just left."

In resignation, Kyle turned to reach for the door handle himself, and Mary pulled her hand back. He winced at her reaction. "Mary, I care for you—for you both."

"You have a poor way of showing it."

"I'd intended to talk to you about it, to tell you the truth. At the time, under the circumstances, it all seemed so logical!"

Mary nodded toward the door. "Under the circumstances now, I think you'd better go."

Kyle released a heavy sigh. "I can't make you understand tonight, but I will. This isn't over, Mary."

He opened the door and left quickly, a snap in his steps as he strode down the sidewalk. Mary closed the door behind him and quickly moved away from the door. She didn't want to hear the sound of his car pulling down the street.

He was wrong. It *was* over. It had to be.

Chapter Eight

The old, beat-up spiral notebook lay in front of her on the glass-topped kitchen table. Mary sat in a wicker chair, hugging down her fourth cup of coffee in an hour. She needed to be awake when Maggie came home.

After a night of pacing, alternately raging at herself for her foolishness and weeping for the same reason, she had very little energy left. The writing in front of her blurred, but it didn't matter. She had it memorized now—every last embarrassing, girlish word, all of which Kyle had obviously taken to be gospel truth. Maggie, too, if the purple fingerprint smudges covering the yellowed diary pages were any indication.

If there was any reason she had thought things could work between her and Kyle now, it was because they were older and supposedly wiser. That was a joke. The stunt he'd pulled was worse than juvenile—to her mind, it bordered on the vicious. Granted, if he had come straight out and asked her about Maggie, she would have been taken aback—even offended—but that would have been nothing compared to the fury and humiliation she now felt.

For weeks she had wondered what Kyle was up to. She had even suspected that he was using Maggie to maneuver himself into *her* life. What an idiot she had been! And how blind. She remembered the times he had asked about Maggie, but she had been too carried away at the thought of his being attracted to her to think twice about his motives. She reddened with shame, then squirmed in her chair. Kyle had probably been laughing at her the whole time.

Her fresh bout of rage renewed her energy somewhat. When she heard her father's pickup as he dropped off Maggie, she took a deep breath. God, this was going to be painful. She squared her shoulders, though, and tried to steel herself to be firm.

Maggie came bursting through the door. "I thought you wouldn't be up, so I told Grandpa not to—"

Her words came to an abrupt end as her eyes alit on the spiral notebook, then traveled up to Mary's stern expression.

"Uh-oh." Maggie shuffled over to the table and sank into a chair. "I only read it a couple of times," she explained defensively.

"You shouldn't have read it at all," Mary said. "This is a diary, Maggie—it's private."

Maggie rolled her eyes. "Oh, Mom, that's so corny." Before Mary could put in her objection, Maggie continued, "Besides, you don't have to be embarrassed or anything. I know all about the stuff that happened."

"You do?"

"Well, I mean, I didn't know until I read it, but it's no big deal." Maggie shrugged her shoulders. "I know all about sex and stuff."

Mary's jaw dropped. "You do?" *Sex* was not a word she had expected to hear coming out of her twelve-year-old's mouth in her presence.

"Mother, get real. They show us films about all that in school. Last year we saw *Your Body, Yourself,* and this year was *Beyond the Birds and the Bees.* They were both about sex."

"Oh?" Mary blinked, struggling to adjust to her daughter's speaking more frankly than she ever would, given the choice. She was also trying to figure out how health films justified reading people's diaries.

"Well, yeah. Mom, you don't know. There are sexually transmitted diseases out there, like gonorrhea and AIDS. People have to be careful. It's not like it was in your time."

"Maggie—"

"And think about all the single mothers, so many of them teenagers. Kids can't live in a vacuum like they used to, Mom. You of all people should know the pitfalls of becoming an unwed mother, since you almost were one."

"Maggie, I think we need to—"

"I don't blame you one bit, Mom," Maggie interrupted. "Kyle was probably even better looking then than he is now. It's just lucky that Dad married you. Lucky for you, at least. But since Kyle's back, I guess everything's worked out for the best anyway."

"Maggie, we need to have a very serious talk."

Maggie nodded. "Don't worry," she assured, "I won't mind having Kyle as a father. I mean, like, it only seems right, since he *is* my father."

Mary took a deep breath. This was even worse than she had expected. Not only had her daughter been maneuvering her toward disaster, she'd apparently created a fictitious reality for herself.

"Maggie, he's not."

Maggie's eyes widened, then she let out an exasperated breath. "Oh, come on, Mom. Like, I always knew that I couldn't have an accountant for a father. I mean, it's just so boring. So when I accidentally read your diary by mistake, it just made sense that K. W. was really my dad. Everybody knows that the human gestation period is nine months, and if you and he...you know...in December, and then I came along nine months later..." She shrugged again. "Well, even Kyle thinks so."

"Not anymore," Mary said.

Maggie stared at her, disbelieving. "You mean—?"

Mary reached across the table and took her daughter's hand. "Oh, Maggie, I'm afraid you're way off on this one."

Panic began to show itself in Maggie's eyes. "So what are you saying?"

Mary looked straight into her eyes. "Kyle's not your father, Maggie."

Maggie nearly jumped out of her chair. "But that can't be right!"

In that moment, Mary realized that this situation went deeper than Maggie's having read her diary, or Kyle's betrayal. It pained her to see how desperately her daughter wanted a father—a living, breathing, cool one. But there was nothing she could do about that, except tell her the truth and hope she came to accept it.

"He isn't," Mary said, shaking her head. "Bill Moore was your father. And I know this is hard for you to understand, since you never knew him, but he was a genuinely wonderful person. Even if he was an accountant."

Maggie's shoulders sagged. "I can't believe it."

"I'm sorry, Maggie," Mary said. She felt her eyes welling with tears and fought them back. "I'm sorry I haven't told you more about your father. I should have, and I will. But just because a person is an accountant, or a secretary, doesn't mean that's all that person is."

"Yeah, but Kyle—"

"I understand how you feel," Mary said. "But his wearing a leather jacket doesn't make him your father."

"Mom," Maggie protested, pointing at the diary, "you wrote in there that you loved Kyle. Dad got maybe five paragraphs in the whole thing."

Mary cringed. Her daughter was annoyingly astute. "The fact is, I was in love with them both." She swallowed against the tight lump that formed in her throat. "But the feelings I had for Kyle were...immature. It was painful for me to realize that."

"Yeah, you sounded pretty upset."

"I was," Mary admitted. "But Bill picked me back up, Maggie. I've always thought you picked up your odd mix of single-mindedness and whimsy from him—that's how he won me over. And for those few months, we were happy together. Had he lived, I imagine we would have gone on being happy."

"Oh." Maggie was so obviously disappointed that Mary couldn't help feeling sorry for her. "I thought you got married because of me."

Mary shook her head. She felt surprisingly calm now that everything was out in the open, except worrying about the confusion Maggie had probably gone through. "I became pregnant right after I married Bill. You were premature, Maggie. It's not out of the ordinary for a baby to come early sometimes, or late."

"I guess I should have thought of that," Maggie said. "I've really messed up this time, haven't I?"

"It's not your fault," Mary said. "I should have told you about all this earlier—about everything. I'm afraid *Beyond the Birds and the Bees* doesn't always cut it when it comes to real life."

"But what about Kyle?" Maggie asked. "You aren't mad at him, are you?"

"I'm not sure about that," Mary lied. She felt like wringing the man's neck, but she suspected that saying so to her daughter would only aggravate the situation. "Right now, I'm just tired. I think I'm going to take a nap until lunch."

"Okay," Maggie said, sighing. She watched Mary get up and walk to the door leading out of the kitchen. "Mom?"

Mary turned. "What is it?"

Maggie cleared her throat. "Does this mean I'm grounded for another couple of months?"

"No, you're not grounded," Mary said, a fond smile tugging at her lips.

Maggie nodded soberly. "I'm sorry I goofed this up so bad."

"We'll talk about it some more this afternoon," Mary promised, then went to her room.

Maggie crossed her arms and sank even lower in her chair. Boy, this was terrible. She couldn't believe Kyle had snitched on her, for one thing. But maybe her mom had figured it out somehow.

What was she going to do now? Her mom didn't fool her one bit. She was steaming mad at Kyle—otherwise, she would have gone ahead and said she wasn't mad at him. And her taking to her bed on a Sunday morning was definitely not a good sign. All in all, it seemed to Maggie that they must have had one knock-down, drag-out fight. And now she'd never see Kyle again.

But she had to! Kyle was her friend, and she knew he still liked her mom. In fact, if he was desperate enough to go to the boring symphony with her, he must like her a lot.

If only her mom didn't get so bent out of shape about dishonesty and all that stuff. Somehow, she had to find a way to make her see that Kyle was still interested...if he still was.

Panic seized her. What if he really didn't want to see them, now that he knew the truth?

There was one way to find out. In a second, she was out the door. She shut it very, very quietly behind her and headed straight for her bicycle. After all, her mom had said she wasn't grounded.

Whoever was knocking at his door at ten o'clock on a Sunday morning—after a night when he'd gotten exactly zippo sleep—had better have a damn good reason for doing it.

Kyle padded down the carpeted stairs, shoving his arms through the armholes of his hastily retrieved robe. He looked like hell, and he knew it. His hair was askew, his eyes were hound-dog red, and he felt a whopper of a headache coming on. If this turned out to be Sam Terry coming to retrieve his yard tools, his blood pressure would probably go off the map.

He swung the front door open in one fast motion, prepared to meet the pest with an intimidating scowl. But the round, anxious blue eyes that looked up into his sent his annoyance in a totally new direction.

Maggie! He hadn't even considered this sticky situation.

"What took you so long?" Maggie asked in what he guessed was a timid voice for her. "Did I wake you up or something?"

Kyle shrugged, then rubbed a hand over his face, trying to get some blood circulating somewhere. "I don't think you should be here, Maggie," he said finally.

"All I've met up with today are cranky old people," Maggie replied, not budging one inch. "Aren't you gonna at least let me come in?"

"I don't know..."

"Mom doesn't know I've come here. She went back to bed."

Lucky Mom, Kyle thought. What on earth was he sup posed to do now? He couldn't just shut the door on her, and he couldn't stand out in his yard with no clothes on talking to a kid.

"Okay," he said with a sigh of defeat. "Come on in."

Maggie crept across the threshold, her neck craning cu riously as she took in his house. "Wow, nice," she said.

"Why don't you help yourself to some orange juice, and I'll meet you out on the patio. Feel free to snoop."

"Okay, but I'd rather have coffee."

"Then be generous and make enough for two."

Maggie nodded and started ambling toward the living room.

"Uh, Maggie?" Kyle said, getting her attention. "Kitch en's the other way."

"You said I could snoop," she protested.

Kyle rolled his eyes. "I thought teenagers were supposed to sleep till noon," he moaned.

"I'm exceptional."

He took the stairs two at a time, jumped in and out of the shower, threw on some clothes and was back downstairs in fifteen minutes. All the while, he dreaded trying to explain the events of last night to Maggie. But when he found her staring in amazement at the drained swimming pool off his patio, he took heart. If he couldn't find words, she surely would.

She looked up at him, disbelief in her eyes. "You do have have a swimming pool."

"I wasn't holding out on you," he said, laughing before taking a sip of coffee. "This is my parents' house."

"They died?" Maggie asked without any signs of awk wardness.

"Yeah, they're both gone now," Kyle said.

"Oh." She stepped away from the swimming pool. " didn't think about your having any." She stared at him then just the slightest trace of regret in her eyes. "I never knew my dad. I guess that's why I got so freaked out. I'm sorry if I messed up things for you."

Kyle let out a heavy breath. "It wasn't your fault, Maggie. I was freaked out, too, I guess. I should've known that you can't lose one family and expect to have another one handed to you on a platter."

Maggie shrugged. "Mom will get over it. I'm sure she will."

Kyle shook his head. "I thought so, too, at first. But now..."

The girl raised her arms in exasperation and let them drop to her sides. "You're just giving up?"

"Not giving up, Maggie, accepting the truth. Your mother was very angry."

Maggie waved off his protest. "Oh, she's mad at me all the time. You can bring her around, I know you can." She sent him a hard stare. "If you want to, that is."

She raised her coffee cup to her lips in challenge. Kyle answered in kind, but he had none of Maggie's certainty about any of this. All he could think of was the look of betrayal in Mary's eyes.

He'd made some mistakes in his life, but this one beat them all. Last night, he had left Mary's house with every thought of doing what Maggie suggested—bringing her around. But once he was back in his big empty house, the magnitude of his blunder had hit him full force.

There was no point being more masochistic than the situation called for. Mary would probably never forgive him for this. He'd be surprised if she didn't hand in her resignation Monday—a lot of good he would have ended up doing her and Maggie in that case.

He sighed again. "Once you've lost someone's trust twice, it's a hard thing to win back."

"I trust you," Maggie said more pleadingly.

"That's another thing," Kyle answered, "I probably should have sent you home immediately. Mary will probably go ballistic when she finds out you were here."

"I won't tell her," Maggie answered simply.

"I will."

Maggie's mouth dropped open. "Why?"

"Not only will I tell her, I'll deliver you to her myself."

"Are you insane?" Maggie asked, incredulous.

Kyle shook his head. "No more lies, Maggie, and no more sneaking around. I was wrong to do what I did, and now, if I'm going to win your mother's friendship back, I've got to be square with her."

"Then you do still like her," Maggie said.

"More than ever," Kyle admitted.

"Yes!" Maggie cried triumphantly. She rocked on her toes happily for a moment, then looked at him, beaming. "This is going to be a piece of cake."

"You think so?" Kyle asked with a skeptical chuckle.

"Oh, yeah." Maggie frowned. "You just need to wear her down—like that thing they talk about in science class. Like what rain does to a granite boulder."

"Erosion?"

"Yeah, that's it," Maggie said excitedly. "I think you should start by sending her some more flowers or something. She seems to like that."

Kyle laughed outright then. "I'll do my best. For now, you'd better bring your bike around so we can load it in the car."

"Okay," Maggie replied reluctantly, "but I still say you're crazy to face her today."

Kyle collapsed on a lawn chair when Maggie disappeared around the side yard. Maggie was right about one thing—he probably did need to gather his wits before seeing Mary this morning. He took a deep drink and shut his eyes pensively.

She was right about the charm thing, too. Mary would see reason eventually, she just needed to be worn down. He had Maggie on his team, evidently. And then he would barrage her with tokens of goodwill. Hauling Maggie back would be his first gesture.

He heard footsteps coming around the house. "Hope that thing fits in the sedan," he said, his eyes refusing to open into the glint of the morning sun.

"Kyle."

His breath caught. The voice sounded like Maggie's, but it wasn't. The tone was deeper, a woman's voice. Mary's voice. Praying that his mind was simply playing tricks on him, he slowly opened his eyes.

Mary loomed over him, a dark silhouette in the brightness. Her balled fists rested on her hips.

Immediately, he sat up and struggled to unfold himself from the chaise longue. "Mary, I—"

"You have a lot of nerve," she interrupted. "You should have called me immediately."

"I know," Kyle explained. "I should have, but she seemed to need to talk to someone." He folded his arms across his chest as their bloodshot eyes made contact. "And I guess I needed to, too."

Mary relaxed her posture somewhat, bringing her arms to her sides. "I'm taking her home now."

"Mary," he said, stopping her with a hand to her arm before she could turn to leave. "I'm sorry about this, I really am."

She looked down at his arm in dismay. "There's no need to apologize. I know you didn't invite her over."

Kyle laughed. "She has a mind of her own."

"Just don't encourage her," Mary said. "Please."

Mary had hoped that he would take the last pleading word as his cue to let go of her arm, but he didn't. He simply continued to stare into her eyes.

She'd been in such a blind panic when she found Maggie missing after noticing the conspicuous silence in the house that she hadn't thought twice before roaring over here. Now she regretted not calling first. His brown eyes seemed as sleep-deprived as her own, and she certainly sympathized with the anguished expression in them. But she shouldn't, she knew she shouldn't.

"I don't want you to even think about leaving Zieglar and Weston," he said finally.

The words surprised her. Not because she hadn't thought about this, but because he had. "I'm not sure about that yet."

"I'm not going to let you go until I have your promise," he said.

"That's not your decision to make."

Kyle took a step closer. "I know I've hurt you, Mary. But don't punish yourself and Maggie because of my foolishness."

Mary frowned. "It's awkward, Kyle . . ."

"It won't be," he promised her. "I'll stay out of your way. At work."

That small tag line made her nervous. "If you'll change that to 'at work and everywhere else,' we'll have a deal," she answered.

Kyle shook his head slowly. "I can't do that."

She rolled her eyes and tugged at her arm in frustration. "Maggie's waiting, Kyle. I really need to go."

"Promise."

"Kyle!"

"I mean it, Mary," he said earnestly, "I care about what happens to you."

"You shouldn't worry," she shot back, "I've been making decisions for myself for a long time."

"But wouldn't life be better if you didn't have to?"

"That would depend on what the alternative was."

Something in her tone made him snap. He closed what little distance there was between them and gathered her in his arms. As his mouth descended on hers, a tiny voice in his head whispered, *Mistake, big mistake.*

But she tasted so good, and she felt so right, even nestled as stiffly as she was against him. In a flash, her hands slid up to the nape of his neck, then fell down to his arms to push away. But the lingering sensation on the skin of his neck where she had so briefly clasped her hands was enough to give him hope. When he finally released her, she jumped back a step, nearly tripping over a lawn chair.

She crossed her arms defiantly. "You shouldn't have done that."

"Why?" he ventured. "Because it reminded you that we care for each other?"

Her eyes squinted. "Care? People who care for each other don't connive and deceive and take the other for a fool, which is what you've done."

"And what would you have felt if I'd simply asked you weeks ago if Maggie was my daughter?"

"Mad as a hornet," Mary admitted, "but at least that would've been honest."

"That kiss just now was as honest as they come. I care for you, Mary."

Mary's mouth dropped open, then abruptly closed. "You said that before," she replied. "Traditional male tactics aren't going to work, Kyle."

She didn't think so, at least. She needed to get away from him, fast, before he actually managed to change her mind. Slowly, she took a few steps backward. "I need to get Maggie home now," she said.

Kyle nodded. "I'll see you tomorrow then." He smiled. "Tell Maggie that the granite is eroding."

Mary raised her brows questioningly, but she wasn't sure she wanted to know what the message really meant. Nor did she care to prolong their meeting. "Goodbye," she said, then turned and left.

After she'd gone, Kyle sank back into a chair and tried to gauge his chances. A piece of cake? He didn't think so. But possible, very possible.

"Okay, so who is it?" Ben asked.

"Some lunatic," Mary replied, staring at the gorgeous arrangement of daisies her co-worker had just brought into her already cluttered office.

"Flowers, candy, season tickets to the symphony..." He shrugged. "None of the lunatics I know are so generous."

Mary laughed stiffly. This routine was becoming pretty tiresome. Kyle had promised to leave her alone at work, and so far he had—at least, she hadn't seen him. But the almost hourly deliveries were beginning to get on her nerves.

"Maybe you just haven't run into the right kind of crazy person. Or maybe I mean the wrong kind." She spotted a memo on her desk that she had just written that morning. "Sorry to cut this short," she said. "I've got to run this by Kyle."

"It's Kyle, isn't it?" Ben said, mischief sparking in his eyes.

"No!" Mary squeaked. "I mean, of course not. Kyle?" She rolled her eyes. "Good heavens."

She left Ben standing in her office doorway and dashed down the hall. Mrs. Hester, Kyle's bulldoggish new secretary, attempted to stop her. "He's busy," she warned.

"Tough." Mary barged past and entered Kyle's office without knocking.

Kyle looked up in surprise when Mary appeared at his desk. He swiveled away from his computer and crossed his arms, his eyes expectant. "Something I can do for you?"

"Yes," Mary huffed. "You can hold up your end of the bargain."

He sent her a questioning glance. "Bargain?"

Mary lowered her voice. "You know what I mean. Sunday you said that you wouldn't bother me at work, but since Monday morning my tiny office has been bombarded with...stuff."

"Tokens of my esteem."

"Kyle!" Her voice rose in frustration.

"I gather you would rather I sent them to your house."

"I would rather you didn't send them at all."

Kyle sighed dramatically and looked at her with brown, boyishly innocent eyes. "I'm not getting through to you at all, then?"

"If you were trying to annoy me, you've succeeded nicely."

Kyle rose and skirted his desk to join her. "All joking aside, Mary." He came so close that she had to take a step back to keep from colliding with him. "You know that's not what I want."

She let out an exasperated breath. "What do you want, Kyle? Visitation rights to your employee's daughter?"

Kyle scowled. "This isn't about Maggie now."

Mary raised a skeptical brow. "She would be surprised to hear it. She asks about you every day."

"Still? After four whole days?" Kyle asked, a smile tugging on his lips. "I'm glad to know I have someone with so much staying power on my team."

Mary rolled her eyes. "Both of you are incorrigible."

"Incorrigibly cute?" Kyle pressed.

"Oh!" She turned on her heel and headed for the door. "No more flowers, Kyle. No candy or tickets or anything else your feverish little brain can cook up." She swung open the door and nodded toward his desk. "Oh, and there's a memo for you."

Kyle laughed as she stormed out. He absently picked up the memo and went to sit down in his chair again. If he'd managed to get Mary into that much of a swivet, he had to be doing something right.

But Mary was correct in saying that he had to decide what he was after. Tomorrow was Friday. He'd have a quiet evening at home to think about it. Maybe he'd even do some work around the house. Or perhaps—and Sam Terry would laugh to hear him say it—yard work was more his speed now.

Chapter Nine

Mary squirmed in her seat during the final scene of *Giant*, wondering how on earth she had managed to survive a James Dean double feature. Soap operas about deep inner turmoil and tragic love were not exactly what she was in the mood for. Not for the first time, she wished Maggie was into something more cathartic, like Errol Flynn pirate movies—with lots of fast action and happy, happy endings.

But Maggie seemed placated, which was cheering in itself. Gone was the "no James Dean" rule, and on this Saturday—just this once, Mary promised herself—they were playing hooky from volunteerism. Maggie was in seventh heaven, and Mary had to admit that she was enjoying herself, too.

What had Maggie called it? Loosening up.

Well, maybe she had loosened up. God knows, she had been as tightly wound as humanly possible in the past week. But after kicking back for two days with Maggie, she felt more relaxed. If it wasn't for the hollow pit in her stomach, she would have sworn that last weekend's fiasco had never happened.

She recognized that hollow feeling from the months after Bill had died. It was grief, or at the very least, the blues. But sitting here in the movie theater, with her enraptured daughter seated next to her, she could easily see the end of her minor depression. She and Maggie could go shopping after the film, then maybe order a pizza tonight. By the end of the weekend, she would probably forget Kyle had ever existed as someone other than just another person at work.

Finally, the music swelled and the lights came up. Mary jumped from her seat and tried to stretch inconspicuously. As her eyes adjusted to the brightness against the hue of the red upholstered interior of the theater, she could make out faces of the other patrons. They all seemed to share the same dazed, glassy-eyed expression. And then her breath caught.

Three rows behind them sat Kyle Weston. After momentarily meeting his gaze, she quickly turned away.

"Ready?" she asked Maggie energetically. Out of the corner of her eye, she caught Kyle sidling closer through the long row of seats behind them.

Maggie let out a heavy, sated breath. "I could stay here forever, I think."

"Yes, well, the double feature's over," Mary sing-songed. She practically hoisted her daughter up by the armpits, which turned out to be a mistake.

"Look, Mom!" Maggie cried out as she stood. "It's Kyle!" She smiled and waved and awkwardly hurdled over her seat to greet Kyle with a heartfelt hug.

Mary hung back, feeling oddly fenced off from all this exuberance by the waist-high row separating them.

Kyle nodded politely at her. "Hiya, Mary," he said, as if addressing a colleague he'd just happened by chance to meet.

His throwaway tone irked Mary for some unfathomable reason. Nevertheless, she took her cue from him and returned his salutation with a stiff smile. "Kyle, I hadn't expected to see you here." She hadn't, although now she asked herself why. Since Kyle knew what he did about Maggie's cinematic taste, she realized that just in coming here she'd set herself up as a sitting duck.

"Yeah, Kyle," Maggie exclaimed guilelessly, "after last Sunday, I never thought I'd see you again."

Mary winced, but Kyle chuckled and made a show of patting down his leather jacket. "Didn't you know? I'm a lifelong James Dean fan."

"Cool."

Cool was exactly the opposite of what Mary was feeling at the moment. In the muted light of the theater, Kyle looked as handsome as ever. The admiration showing on Maggie's face unexpectedly bubbled up inside of her, too; not just for Kyle's all-American good looks, either. In public he just seemed to ooze charisma and self-confidence.

She caught the devilish glint in his eyes, a hint that he knew full well he was getting to her. And he was, of course, the arrogant man. But only because she was letting him, and she would soon put a stop to that.

"Well," she said brusquely, "Maggie and I need to be shoving off."

"I'll walk you out," Kyle said.

Repressing a frustrated sigh, Mary snatched her purse from her seat and followed Maggie and Kyle to the lobby. The two of them still got along like gangbusters. Much to Mary's dismay, she found herself questioning the possibility that Kyle had come to the movies just to bump into them. How would he have predicted they'd be there? The double feature was running through the weekend, and as far as he knew, Maggie was still grounded.

Whatever his motives were, Mary was forced to reach a disturbing conclusion. While the blues might go away eventually, Kyle himself might be harder to get rid of.

She hoped he would stay for the next film, but he walked out of the building with them. They all stopped at Mary's car, Maggie and Kyle seeming reluctant to part ways. Mary, on the other hand, wanted nothing more than to jump in the car and make tracks. She breezed past the trunk, where they were both hanging back.

"Well," she said with a brightness she didn't feel as she unlocked her door, "I suppose I'll see you at work Monday, Kyle." There, she thought, that sounded very cordial, very professional.

"This is a real bummer," Maggie whined, seeing that her hopes were being dashed again. "I'll never get to see Kyle."

He gave her a playful punch on the arm. "I wouldn't be so sure of that," he countered with a wink at Mary.

"Really?" Maggie asked, her face lighting up. She looked from one grown-up to the other in wishful speculation.

Mary started to protest. Really, it was criminal of Kyle to get the girl's hopes up. But Kyle cut off her objections, placing his hands squarely on Maggie's shoulders and explaining soberly, "I told you that I'd go to your gross ballet recital."

"Oh, yeah." Maggie tried in vain to hide her disappointment. "The gross recital."

"Maggie," Mary warned. While playing father, Kyle could at least have tried to make some headway toward improving Maggie's attitude toward after-school activities.

"I wouldn't mind if you skipped the recital, if you'd promise to give me another motorcycle lesson." Maggie's tone was pleading, and though the words were directed to Kyle, she was looking straight at Mary.

A long silence followed the request. Kyle also stared plaintively at Mary, although when he detected her inflexibility on this point, there was also understanding in his eyes. Mary was grateful for that, at least.

"I don't know, Maggie," Kyle joked. "I think you've about mastered the ten-miles-an-hour crawl. Your mother will probably want you to wait a few years before moving on to hot-rodding."

Maggie rolled her eyes. "Years? Try a few decades."

"I think we'd better go," Mary said, suddenly feeling like the world's wettest blanket. "We have to stop off for groceries." The two woebegone faces that met that last pitiful excuse tugged at her.

Was she being unreasonable? The pair of them had been plotting against her for weeks; now, even after the truth had come out, it suddenly seemed impossible for her to take the moral high ground. Or, rather, she was finding little satisfaction in taking it.

Kyle gave Maggie a warm pat on the back. "See you later, Maggie," he said. He smiled at Mary, opened his mouth to say something similar to her, then hesitated.

In that split second, Mary's heart leaped to her throat. She could read the intention in his eyes, but felt helpless to evade him. Short of vaulting over the minivan parked next to her, there was no escape. He saw her dilemma and responded quickly.

"What the hell," he muttered hoarsely. Closing the few feet between them almost instantaneously, he gathered Mary into his arms for a brief, drugging kiss.

Maggie gasped. Mary tried but failed to capture any breath at all. Kyle let out an almost inaudible groan and then wrenched himself away.

"Catch you later, Mary," he said jauntily. Mary's dazed eyes met his for a brief moment, and then he walked away, stopping only to tweak Maggie on the chin.

Maggie nearly collapsed against the trunk of the car. "Oh, Mom!" she exclaimed. "He's so cool I could die!"

Mary wanted to die, but for entirely different reasons. Still stunned, she watched Kyle's retreating back as he strolled toward the theater.

What had he done that for? In broad daylight, and in front of her daughter, too! The impropriety of it shocked her, not to mention the volcanic feelings inside her the kiss had left in its wake. Although, looking at Maggie, Mary discerned that the girl was neither repelled nor horrified. Enraptured was more like it.

"You've got to marry him, Mom," Maggie begged. "Or at least sleep with him."

"Maggie!" Mary had a good mind to go running to the PTA with complaints about those blasted sex films Maggie had seen. She just didn't know how many more of these episodes she could take before becoming completely unhinged.

"Oh, heck." Maggie reluctantly trudged toward the passenger side of the car. "If you weren't such an old lady, you'd know that's what you want."

"That's enough!" Mary snapped, getting in the car. As she fastened her seat belt and pulled out of the parking lot, she just stopped herself clucking her tongue in disapproval. That, of course, was what a true old lady would have done.

She hoped that by the time she really was old, she'd have better sense than to get herself into another mess like this one. Maybe by then, she would have a handle on the myriad sensations that roiled through her just by being held by a pair of lean, muscular arms, or by looking into coffee-brown eyes. Until then, however, she'd have to deal with her idiocy.

"That wasn't what you think," Mary explained finally as they approached a red light.

"I don't know," Maggie said. "It looked pretty much like a kiss to me."

"It was." Mary cleared her throat. "But it wasn't indicative of anything serious. I hope you understand that."

Maggie shook her head. "It happened just like in the movies," she said in a dreamy voice.

It had, hadn't it? Mary thought wistfully. Then she gave herself a mental shake. "This isn't a movie, it's my life."

"Oh, brother." Maggie hunkered down low in her seat and crossed her arms. "Don't I know it!"

"I'm serious, Maggie," Mary persisted. "I know this might seem confusing to you, but kisses in real life don't always carry so much weight. I mean, adults sometimes do foolish things without thinking about them."

Maggie tilted her head and regarded her mother skeptically. "You look all shook up, Mom. That must mean something."

"Humph." Mary pressed the accelerator. "It means I'd better learn to leap over tall minivans in a single bound."

They drove the rest of the way to the grocery store in silence. As much as she tried to convince herself otherwise, Mary had to admit that Maggie's point was well-taken. She did feel all shaken up inside. She only hoped that she could avoid Kyle long enough to settle back down again. Permanently.

What did other people do with pizza boxes? They didn't fit in the garbage can, and if you left them in the fridge until garbage day, it was a sure bet you'd forget and they would sit in there getting crustier and crustier for weeks.

This was Mary's dilemma as she sat at her kitchen table that evening. And she had to admit that as problems went, it wasn't too stressful.

She was relaxed again. She'd punted that afternoon's shopping trip idea. Having so recently seen her idol—*idols*—Maggie would have hounded her unmercifully about getting a leather jacket. While Mary could feel her will bending on this point, her wallet was as unyielding as ever. Sometime before Maggie was eighteen, she promised herself, she would present her with one of those infernal things.

Maggie had managed to bully her into watching *Rebel Without a Cause* when they got home, however. Which added up to all three of that man's feature films in one day. Mary shook her head. She wished James Dean would have lived to make a few more movies at least. These few were becoming tedious.

The doorbell rang, and from the recesses of the house, she heard Maggie's familiar cry, "I got it!" Mary slid out of her seat and walked through the dining room toward the front hall.

"Kyle!"

"Hey, Maggie. Is your mother home?"

Mary stopped in her tracks at the sound of Kyle's voice. She wanted to run and hide, for Maggie to lie and say she wasn't home. Why, why did he have to come after her just when she felt as if her equilibrium had been restored?

"Mom!" Maggie cried, then saw her a few feet away. "Oh, here she is."

Kyle stepped inside and Maggie closed the door behind him. "Mary," he said, nodding.

"Oh, Kyle! We just watched the movie you gave us." Maggie's eyes lit up and she looked over at Mary. "Hey, Mom, why don't we watch it again, with Kyle?"

Mary didn't think she could have objected strenuously enough to that idea, but luckily she didn't have to. Kyle shook his head and put a hand on Maggie's shoulder.

"Actually, Maggie," he said in a quiet voice, "I need to talk to your mother alone."

Mary hoped her dismay wasn't as evident as Maggie's disappointment was. "Man," Maggie said. "I hate it when this happens."

"Sorry," Kyle apologized.

"Does this mean bad news?" Maggie pressed.

Kyle's eyes zoomed in on Mary, piercing in their intensity. "I hope not, Maggie. I hope not."

"Kyle, I—"

Maggie cut off Mary's protest. "Okay, I'm going to my room now."

She left them standing in the hallway. "Would you like some coffee?" Mary asked hesitantly, hoping that he wouldn't.

"No," he said. "I just want to talk to you."

They stood staring at each other for a moment. She could have used a cup of coffee, she realized. A big strong one. "I guess we should go to the living room," she said finally, steeling herself for whatever was coming next.

Kyle's somber mood disturbed her as he led the way to the next room. When he turned to her, it struck her that she had never seen him so subdued before, so deadly serious.

"I won't prolong this, Mary," he said, reaching into his jacket. "There's something that I want you to have."

He pulled out a tiny, square package wrapped in bright yellow paper and handed it to her.

Mary held up her hands. "I can't take that."

"You haven't even seen what's inside."

"Kyle, I can't."

He reached over and grabbed her right hand, then placed the box in her palm. "Open it," he insisted.

Mary huffed out a breath and started ripping at the paper. When it revealed a velveteen jewelry box, she looked up at Kyle in surprise.

"Go ahead," he prodded.

Closing her eyes, she flipped up the top. When she looked down, a chunky diamond solitaire shone up at her. Mary gaped at the brilliance of the gem.

"You told me I needed to decide what I was after," Kyle explained quickly as Mary continued to stare at the ring. "I have. I want you and Maggie. I want us to be a family."

Mary tried to take in his words even as her thoughts raced. Marriage. He was asking her to marry him. Wasn't he?

She looked up. "You mean . . ."

Kyle smiled for the first time since entering the house. "Will you marry me?"

Mary cut her eyes back down to the ring, her pulse racing. If Kyle had asked her to sprout wings and fly, she couldn't have been more surprised. Married, to Kyle Weston?

Funny, she would have given anything to have him ask her thirteen years ago. Now, she was just suspicious. Not a word had he spoken about love, and even if he had, could she believe him? Twice she had placed her trust in Kyle, and twice he had pulled the rug out from under her hopes. Diamonds couldn't change that.

Before she could think any more, she snapped the box closed and held it out to him. "I'm sorry, Kyle."

His face paled. "Mary, this is serious."

"I know," she said. "But I can't accept this, or your proposal."

He shoved his fists in his pockets, pointedly not taking the ring back. Mary sighed, but was just as determined to return it. "I'm not going to change my mind, Kyle."

"Look," he explained, "I know this might seem hasty to you, but I've thought carefully about us. I want to be with you."

I want. Mary heard little beyond those two words. Nowhere had he mentioned what she might want, or what would happen when in a few months, or maybe even years, Kyle decided his desires lay elsewhere.

"Two weeks ago you mentioned a woman named Cindy Sellars," Mary said. "And before that, when I was your secretary, I got calls from any number of young women to put through to your office."

"Those women didn't mean anything to me," Kyle protested.

"Is that what you told them?" she asked. "You've only been back in Dallas for a little over a month."

"I know I might seem like something of a . . . playboy to you, but I'm not. I've changed since I've come back. I don't want that kind of life for myself anymore."

"I'm sorry, Kyle," Mary said again, more sadly. "I don't want to be your experiment in domesticity. I might have once, but things have changed. I've raised a girl on my own and supported myself alone for almost my whole adult life."

"I know this seems improbable," he tried explaining once more, "but I never expected that I'd want to get married. Suddenly, after I came home, I realized I was too long in the tooth to go on as I was. I wanted something more permanent, like my own parents had. I'm ready to settle down."

Mary held back a smirk. "I don't want to be what somebody settles for, Kyle."

"That's not what I meant and you know it," he shot back. Then he sighed. "I guess what you're saying is that you still don't trust me."

She continued to stare at him, holding out the box. It felt as though they were playing a tug-of-war in reverse with the ring, and Mary was quickly becoming exhausted. "I don't want to marry you," she said flatly.

Kyle knew he must look stupefied standing there gaping at her, but in truth, he was stumped. He'd expected his proposal to be greeted with, if not joy, at least a little more indecision. "You don't even want to think about it?"

Leaving Kyle's proposal dangling while she tried to make up her mind would be a strain, especially on Maggie. It was best that she wrapped up this episode in her life.

"I don't need to," she replied.

Kyle reached forward and finally took the box. She couldn't be any plainer than that, he supposed. Frustration started to turn to anger as he shoved the ring into his pocket.

"I guess that's it, then," he said in a clipped voice.

Mary nodded.

"I'm sorry to have bothered you," he said bitterly as he turned from her. "I can see myself out."

He could hear Mary following behind him, but he said nothing more. Once he was safely in the privacy of his car, he sank down on the seat and slapped his palm on the steering wheel.

Damn! Of all the stupid ideas he'd ever had, this one was the topper. At age thirty-five, to offer himself up to some woman who had given every indication that she wanted nothing to do with him was the epitome of dumb moves. She'd just turned him down cold! Without a qualm, apparently.

He slapped the steering wheel again, inadvertently touching off the horn. Surprised by the honking noise, he turned on the ignition and quickly hurried down the street. He wanted to put distance between him and Mary as fast as possible.

When he was out of her neighborhood, he began to think more logically, and the weight of the box in his jacket pocket began to feel less burdensome. Maybe Mary had done him a favor. She was probably right, after all. You couldn't teach an old dog new tricks.

The cliché settled uneasily in his system. If he didn't learn new tricks, and he was tired of the old ones, what else was there?

His father's house loomed even bigger and emptier as he pulled into the driveway. Soon he would have to decide whether to put the monster on the real estate market. He hated to do it, but living there alone was a waste of space. Not to mention lonely.

He trudged up to the side door and let himself into the kitchen. Automatically he walked over to the fridge and peered inside. There was nothing in it but milk, eggs, a few bottles of beer and an old pizza box from weeks past that he kept forgetting to take out to the garbage. Typical bachelor fridge.

Kyle sighed, grabbed the milk and sat down at the kitchen table. Maybe proposing to Mary hadn't been a mistake. It had been worth a shot, at least. But since no big wedding was going to take place, he had to find something else to do with himself.

At one time, he would have considered going out and finding himself a new girl. Now all he could think of to do was work. Work was a responsibility, at least, and one that he could control.

At the very edge of the mirrored wall in the studio of Madame Jarde's School of the Ballet, Maggie and Winona sat hunched beneath the long wooden bar, watching the butterflies rehearse. Having been relegated to play the wind for the recital despite her big push, Maggie wasn't due on for another ten minutes at least. More, if she figured in all the fits and starts caused by Lisa Dugan's clumsiness. But Lisa Dugan was cute and had a perfect attendance record, so of course she was the lead butterfly.

"One week," Maggie moaned miserably. "What if Kyle actually does come?"

"You said he and your mom haven't talked for weeks," Winona replied. "But if he did happen to show up, wouldn't that be good?"

"Are you nuts?" Maggie hissed at her friend. It was hard to talk low enough so that they wouldn't be heard over the music. "If you came all the way to a gross ballet recital to watch some kid who wasn't even your daughter, and you saw her being the crummy old wind, what would you think?"

"I dunno," Winona said, puzzled.

"You'd think, 'Thank God that kid isn't mine,' that's what."

"Guess you're right." Winona drew her knees up to her chest. "At least you aren't the rain, though."

Maggie sighed. It was all so unfair. Even though she could jump higher than any kid in the class, Madame Jarde still didn't think she had the skill to be a butterfly. The woman was obviously prejudiced. Nevertheless, poor Winona did have a bum deal, having to be the rain.

At that moment, petite Lisa Dugan, so blond and cute that Maggie wanted to slap her, tripped. She and Winona covered their grins.

"Maybe you should be glad you aren't a butterfly, Maggie."

"Humph," Maggie mumbled glumly.

"Maybe there's more you could do with the wind."

The butterflies floated gracefully across the room in perfect unison, pink and perfect, lovingly underscored by Beethoven's sixth symphony. In a few moments, to the crash of cymbals, Maggie would come on and chase them all away, heralding the storm that would be performed by the older students in the Saturday class.

A smile suddenly lit up Maggie's face.

"What's wrong?" Winona asked. She'd seen that devilish smile before. It usually meant that they were about to do something that would get them into big trouble.

"Nothing," Maggie said. "I think I've just decided what kind of wind I want to be. Remember that film we saw on Isadora Duncan, the dancer who strangled herself on her scarf?"

Winona looked at her skeptically. "I'm not going to get in trouble for this, am I?"

"No."

"Phew. I thought you were going to strangle Lisa Dugan."

Maggie rolled her eyes. "Good grief! No, I just decided what kind of wind I want to be—the wild wind. I mean, I can't just be a wimpy wind when Kyle's gonna be out there watching."

"I don't know, Maggie," Winona said. "Don't you think you ought to give up thinking about Kyle and your mom?"

Maggie shook her head resolutely. "Something could still happen, especially if Kyle comes to the recital. That's why I've got to make a definite impression."

"You're scaring me."

"Don't worry, I'll have it under control." Maggie jutted her chin forward stubbornly. "I have to do something."

"I hope it works," Winona put in sympathetically.

"It's got to," Maggie said. "It's just got to." She attempted to put the matter out of her mind and waited for her cue.

Chapter Ten

Strauss's "Emperor Waltz" reverberated through the dark room, punctuated with slightly off-pitch squeaks marking the three-four tempo. On screen, the panorama of a Swiss castle came into view across the glorious mountain vista. The camera slowly moved in, across the castle's manicured lawns, through the palatial entrance, down marbled hallways. The music swelled as a pair of double doors opened wide, revealing a lavish throne room. At the end of a long red carpet lounged a cocker spaniel mutt garbed in a purple robe with a gold crown comically askew on his head. The dog sniffed, and at the bottom of the screen appeared a crystal goblet enticingly filled with dog food.

"When your pet demands royal treatment, the only possible choice is Canine Gourmet."

Snickers from the small audience drowned out the rest of the ad, but even so, it was obvious to Mary that she had not disgraced herself. Sitting next to her, Ben Sykes elbowed her in the ribs, nodding toward Mr. Zieglar in the next row. The old man had a smile on his face. Mary was filled with pride and not a little relief.

And something else, too—disappointment, almost. Now that the project had been successfully completed, she felt at a loss. Working with Ben on that commercial was what had kept her going these past few weeks. Now she again found that there was a hole in her life, a gaping emptiness to remind her that something was missing.

"Not bad," Zieglar pronounced as someone flicked on the lights. "I don't think we'll have much trouble selling that to Hadley."

"Hopefully not to the rest of the world, either," Ben put in.

Zieglar came over and clapped Mary and Ben on their backs. "Not bad at all." He winked jovially at Mary and led the procession out of the conference room.

Mary had gathered her things and was almost to the door before she noticed Kyle, sitting alone in the back row. The look on his face told her that the music from the commercial had brought back memories of their ill-fated date. He wasn't smiling, though.

She took a deep breath and squared her shoulders. Now was as good a time as any to tell him of her plans. It was just too difficult having to get up every day, knowing that she would see Kyle at some point during work. Not only that, but she speculated that he had only assigned her to work for Ben by mistake, or through cowardice. He'd really wanted to talk to her about Maggie that night at the Brass Kettle, but he'd lost his nerve.

The whole scenario was too humiliating, too unsettling. Her best bet was simply to bow out and find another job.

Kyle had expected her to walk away without a word. Strains of that waltz were still playing in his head. He couldn't help remembering how Mary had looked tha night, with her hair swept back and a blue dress outlining every feminine curve on her body.

Now she wore a square-cut, dark gray suit. She looked beautiful but tired. The way he felt. Weeks of seeing her every day but having to maintain a distant, polite demeanor with her had taken their toll on him. And if he could judge by Mary's pale, thinner face, she was having the same problems sleeping at night that he was.

Kyle slowly stretched and stood. Congratulations had to be extended, of course, and he was sincerely glad for Mary. But he also wanted to tell her of his plans. He owed it to her not to let her find out secondhand.

He reached out his hand, and hesitantly Mary took it. An electric current seemed to shoot up his arm from the contact, and both of them pulled back at once.

"Congrats," Kyle said, smiling awkwardly. "I especially liked your choice of music."

"It's a common enough tune," Mary replied defensively. She winced at her sharp tone. Why had she nearly snapped his head off over a piece of music?

Kyle dug his fists into his pockets. "Listen, Mary..."

Mary cut him off. "I'm sorry, Kyle, I didn't mean to be so curt. It's just...well, there's something I should tell you."

"I wanted to talk to you, too."

"Please, Kyle," Mary said, "I was just going to let you know that I've started looking for a new job."

Kyle's eyes widened. "Here, in Dallas?"

"Yes."

He let out a heavy breath. "You shouldn't have to do that."

"But I want to," Mary pleaded. "Not just because of us, although I have to admit that's a problem. It's more than that. I need to move on, I think."

"But you've worked here for almost fifteen years."

Mary let out a light laugh. "I know. I think I might be in a rut."

Her lightened tone relaxed Kyle somewhat. "Listen, Mary, I know that it's been tense around here lately. But the truth is, you don't have to leave because of me. I've decided to return to California."

Mary suppressed a gasp. "California?" The news, which should have been heartening, took her by surprise. "But you just got here!"

Kyle shrugged. "I didn't move back under the best of circumstances," he said. "And then, maybe I went a little overboard with the following-in-my-father's-footsteps routine."

"Who'll take over your end of the business?"

"I'm not sure," Kyle said, rubbing his chin thoughtfully. In truth, he didn't like to think about it, either. His plans were still nascent in his mind. He certainly wasn't ready to pick a replacement. "I haven't thought all this through yet. I just wanted you to hear about my moving from me, not the office grapevine."

Mary nodded and folded her arms across her chest. The hollowness inside had just expanded to capacity. Feeling so devastated by his leaving was unreasonable—she'd always suspected he would. But her sadness went deeper than his just leaving Dallas. He was leaving *her* again, too.

What did she expect? She'd rebuffed him as firmly as she knew how, and she wasn't vain enough to believe that a man would pursue her indefinitely with no encouragement on her part. This time, she was the one running away from commitment.

"I'll be sorry to see you go," she said, but she was too frightened to look him in the eye.

There was a pause as she stared at Kyle's pants leg, and then she heard his soft, deep voice. "Will you, Mary?"

Her breath caught. For a brief moment, she could see how things might work out between them. Maybe, if she swallowed her pride for a fraction of a second, she could make Kyle understand that she needed time to learn to trust again. She could tell him that she didn't want him to go to California because she'd changed her mind about marrying him. It wasn't too late. Yet.

She swallowed, but her pride remained firmly entrenched. Over the past weeks, she suddenly remembered, Kyle hadn't asked even the most perfunctory of personal questions. His behavior toward her had been almost identical to Mr. Zieglar's, not that of a man pining. His offer of marriage might not even still stand.

Looking into his eyes, she answered simply, "Everyone here will miss you. Especially Ben."

Especially *Ben?* Kyle steeled himself against the pain that jolted through him. If Mary had belted him in the gut with a two-by-four, the effect couldn't have been any more stinging.

He tried in the next second to regain his composure. In the best way she knew how, Mary was letting him know that she hadn't changed her mind about marriage. Not that he'd expected her to...well, maybe he clung to an unlikely hope that she would. But what he'd hoped and whether she meant her comment as a dig or not was immaterial now. Her message had come through loud and clear.

A smirk crossed his lips. "I'll miss Ben, too," he said with a touch of bitterness.

Mary closed her eyes. "I'm sorry, I didn't mean—"

"I know what you meant," he replied, his clipped voice cutting her off. A conference room was no place to be having this discussion, anyway. He should have gone by her house—no, she wouldn't have liked that, either. Maybe there was no good time or place to have a discussion of this nature.

"I just wanted you to know that you didn't have to leave because of me," Kyle said. "You've become an important person to this company, Mary. We'd hate to lose you."

Tit for tat, he thought, watching her eyes register the standard company patter he'd just given her. Her disappointment didn't make him feel any better, but maybe later his pride would thank him. He wasn't going to beg at this stage of the game, or stand around explaining that he wasn't just another playboy fleeing the prospect of being tied down. He'd given her the rope, after all, and she had thrown it right back in his face.

"Thank you," Mary replied in a dull voice.

Kyle looked in her eyes, briefly wondering whether she might be disappointed that he hadn't been kinder, or even asked her if she had changed his mind. But it didn't matter now.

He glanced at his watch. "I've got to run," he lied. "See you later, Mary."

Mary barely had time to raise her hand in a small wave before he was gone. She slumped down into the chair on the end of the nearest row. Somehow, almost instinctively, she knew that she'd just made the mistake of her life.

In retrospect, her handling of the situation seemed all wrong. Why had she been so curt, so callous? Given her remark about Ben, she could hardly blame Kyle for answering in kind. Still, his tone had stung.

Unfortunately, it was still early in the day, and there was work to be done. Mary pulled herself out of the chair and ambled slowly toward her new office. She stopped at the door, looking inside at the small room. Kyle's flowers of weeks before were long since gone, and now the primary adornment in the room was her photograph of Maggie.

Maggie, who looked older and maturer with each passing day.

Her daughter always chided her for being so rigid. Now Mary knew why. For all her pride, do-gooding and careful planning, she wouldn't call her life a success at this point. Maggie was perhaps the bright spot, but soon she would be grown up and out on her own.

Well, maybe not *too* soon, but the prospect was close enough at hand to make Mary wonder as she sat down at her desk. In years to come, would this be one of those "if only" days she would look back upon with regret? To borrow a phrase from Maggie, she'd blown it. Bad. In a split second while talking to Kyle, she'd thrown away a chance at happiness with both hands.

His office was only down the hallway, she thought. She'd barged in enough times before—why not now?

But she remained firmly rooted to her chair. Doubts still lingered in her mind... and fear. Maybe if she was given another opportunity with Kyle, she'd handle herself better. Unfortunately, as far as Kyle went, she was afraid her time for opportunity had come and gone.

Butterflies fluttered in Mary's stomach as well as on the stage in front of her, where a host of twelve-year-olds in pink tights flitted about to Beethoven's *Pastoral Symphony*. Where on earth was Maggie? Her daughter had been very secretive about her part in the recital, and Mary suspected that her conspicuous absence from the butterflies had something to do with all those skipped classes.

As her insides tied themselves in knots, Mary fretted about having made Maggie persevere in an activity she so obviously didn't enjoy. How could she have entrusted her one and only child to that terrible Madame Jarde? The woman even scared *her!* And how would it affect Maggie now to be cast out from the other twelve-year-olds' routine?

Her nerves became more ragged as the dance went on. What a fool she'd been. Maggie had never asked for these lessons! She'd had them forced on her, and today they were both paying for it.

Now she wished she could undo the darned lessons and take Maggie home. They could make messy, buttery popcorn and shove *Rebel Without a Cause* into the tape player. Hadn't she just been bragging to Kyle how smart Maggie was? She didn't need such an overly structured routine...neither of them did.

Wanting to undo was a feeling that was becoming quite familiar to Mary. If possible, she would have gladly rewound the past month of her life. Even if she could just go back one week, to the conference room, or further, when Kyle had asked her to marry him...to the moment when she should have thrown herself into his arms and said yes.

Funny, she now equated Kyle with security, when that was the very reason she'd refused him. She'd been afraid he wouldn't stick, that he'd tire of them and tromp off to California again. And now that's exactly where he was going. Even so, at this moment she couldn't help thinking that if Kyle was here, she wouldn't be sitting in an auditorium full of beaming, jittery parents and their little leotarded angels. Or butterflies, rather. Surely Kyle would have had the sense to prevent this terrible thing from happening.

The music decrescendoed, and with the change in tone, Mary's stomach lurched. She anxiously looked around the hall, toward the doors, scoping out an escape route if she needed to faint, or scream, or upchuck. In her frenzied search, her gaze lit on a shadowy figure beneath one of the exit signs.

Kyle.

Of course, Mary thought. He'd promised Maggie that he would attend the gross recital—and it was gross, she realized now. True to his word, he was here for her.

Before she could look away, Kyle sent her a shy, nervous wave. He began creeping around the back of the auditorium toward her. The seat next to her was empty, and Kyle slid into it. Surprisingly, Mary wasn't at all disturbed by his closeness, or the fact that their legs brushed in the confines of the narrow aisle. She needed him too much to worry about things like that now.

What did shock her were the tiny beads of perspiration on his brow, and the way his white knuckles grasped the arms of his chair. He was a nervous wreck!

They looked at each other, and acknowledging each other's anxiety, they laughed silently. In a gesture that brought gratefulness and untold comfort to Mary's heart, Kyle took her hand in his and squeezed it firmly.

This wasn't the time to think things through, to consider whether Kyle's being here was a good or not-so-good thing. Or even whether this was the opportunity that she had been pining for. All her attention was focused on the stage. But somehow, knowing that Kyle was here made her feel safer. They were a cheering section, almost like a—

Kyle leaned in. "I loaned her my leather jacket," he whispered to her.

This was news to Mary. How did leather fit in with graceful winged insects? Her stomach flopped over again.

And then the butterflies began quivering and shaking to the change in the music's tone. Mary's heart slammed against her chest as Maggie at last appeared. She was wearing Kyle's leather jacket, dramatic dark eye makeup and what appeared to be every single one of Mary's scarves tied around her neck.

As her daughter leaped across the stage, the other dancers scattered. Suddenly, Mary understood. Maggie was the wind—a disruptive, malevolent wind. Apparently—ironically—her lack of technical skill had resulted in a solo, and she was playing it to the hilt. She was especially zestful as she chased one butterfly in particular, the perky little blond lead butterfly, off the stage.

Mary began to relax. Feeling Kyle's hand squeeze hers again and glancing at the calm, attentive faces of the other parents, she decided that all her worrying was for nothing. After all, what could happen at a gross ballet recital? She'd just been unprepared. She took another gulp of air and exhaled slowly.

And then, as Maggie finished one of her more spectacular leaps, she landed on a piece of scarf. The audience gasped. As if in slow motion, Mary watched her daughter's foot slide out from under her and her body soar through the air in an almost horizontal position. With a sound somewhere between a thump and a slap, Maggie's backside hit the floor.

Mary and Kyle rocketed out of their seats simultaneously. On stage, Maggie did not get up, but started crawling toward the wings. Kyle looked at Mary.

"Let's go," he said.

His hand still grasping hers, he led her around the seats toward one of the doors. They sped through a maze of corridors and finally found the stage entrance. Madame Jarde was there to greet them, although she had her hands full getting Maggie off and Winona, dripping in silver tinsel for her part as the rain, on.

"Holy Moses, Maggie!" Winona exclaimed. "I told you not to steal all those scarves!"

"Vas!" Madame Jarde commanded Winona as she tugged Maggie from view of the audience. *"Vite,* Winona, already you have missed your cue."

"Sorry, Maggie." Winona sighed. "I guess the show must go on." The girl took a halfhearted, shimmering hop and disappeared onto the stage.

Maggie pushed herself up against the wall with a groan, then gave her mother and Kyle a sly grin. "Sorry," she said.

"Eh, bien!" Madame Jarde turned on Mary. "As well she should be sorry. What is this leather and scarves?"

"Are you okay, Maggie?" Mary crouched beside her and instinctively felt her forehead.

"Mom," Maggie said, rolling her eyes. "I didn't get a fever from falling on my butt."

Mary wasn't so sure. Maggie definitely looked unwell.

"I'm sorry I wasn't in proper costume, Madame Jarde," Maggie apologized, confirming Mary's opinion that she truly was ill.

The Frenchwoman was apparently not moved by the contrite words. "Madame Moore, this is what I mean. Your daughter, she was supposed to be *le vent,* not *le—le hoodlum.*"

"Hoodlum!" Mary cried indignantly.

"What will we do with such a girl? The child is *impossible!*"

"We will take her to the doctor, that's what!" Mary snapped. Whether from nerves, fright or old-fashioned parental pride, she refused, finally, to let this woman bully her. "And next year, we will enroll her in *modern* dance. Anybody in their right mind could tell that Maggie was the most talented, most artistically expressive one on that stage!"

"Geez, Mom," Maggie said under her breath.

"And furthermore, I thought her costume was just right," Mary continued. "She might have stolen the scarves from my bureau without permission, but I thought they looked terrific. And as soon as she's able, I'm taking her out to buy a leather jacket!''

Maggie gasped in disbelief. Even Kyle felt his breath catch. He'd been hanging back, watching the scene unfold with a twinge of admiration for Mary. Now he tugged on her arm, a little afraid that the two women would resort to fisticuffs if he didn't get Mary out of there soon.

"Would you like me to pull your car around?" he asked.

"You came!" Maggie exclaimed. She'd been so riveted by her mother's defense that she hadn't even noticed Kyle.

"I wouldn't have missed this for the world," Kyle replied, and Maggie sensed that he meant more than just the stupid dancing.

Mary fished in her purse for her car keys, but Maggie interrupted her. "I can walk, Mom. It's not that bad."

Kyle and Mary each took one of Maggie's arms and hoisted her up. Supported by one adult at each side, she started leading them out. "Guess I'll miss the curtain call," she said to Madame Jarde.

The woman raised an unrelenting eyebrow and hurrumphed loudly.

As soon as they were out of earshot, Kyle whispered, "But I bet you won't miss her."

The three of them laughed conspiratorially and limp-walked out of the auditorium together.

"A bruised backside," Kyle mused as he stretched out on the top step of Mary's front porch in the twilight. "Not bad for such a spectacular fall."

Mary chuckled. "Maggie never does do things in a small way." She perched on the step below him. Inside, her daughter was laid out on the living room couch in happy invalidism, having been stuffed with chocolate ice cream and parked in front of a James Dean movie.

"But you were the real hero," Kyle said.

Mary smiled. "I won't feel like one in a few days, when I have to shell out the bucks for one of those jackets."

Kyle laughed with her for a moment, then added, "Just think about Madame What's-her-name. It'll be easy."

"Oh!" Mary bristled just remembering their quarrel. "I wanted to deck her."

"I know," Kyle said, chuckling.

"If there's one thing I learned today, it's that I'm never, never going to make people do what they don't want to do. Myself included."

"Like sweating it out in the audience of a ballet recital?"

Mary nodded. "I thought I was going to have a heart attack before that thing ended."

"When Maggie tripped on her scarf, I almost did," Kyle admitted.

They sat in silence for a moment, both recalling the chilling moment when Maggie had lost her footing. Mary cringed. In those few seconds, she had seen the past twelve years pass before her eyes—the best times, not the troubled ones. In the face of disaster, no problems Maggie had ever caused could match the joy she'd brought. And somehow, maybe just because he had been sitting next to her, holding her hand, Kyle at that moment had seemed integral to her happiness.

"Your being there today meant a lot to Maggie," Mary said more seriously.

She thought for a moment. The thread of camaraderie between her and Kyle seemed so fragile, she hesitated to say anything to sever it. Then she remembered all her wishful thinking about opportunities missed. Maybe this was the chance she'd been hoping for.

"It meant a lot to me, too," she added softly.

Kyle's hands settled on her shoulders, and she could have sworn she heard a sigh of relief behind her. She craned her neck to look into his gorgeous eyes.

"I have a confession to make," he said. "I didn't just attend that thing because I'd promised Maggie."

"No?"

He shook his head. "See, I've been fixing up my yard around my house—in case I decided to sell it. But it looked so nice this morning that I just didn't have the heart to meet my real estate agent for the appointment I had scheduled. I called her and canceled. Then I went to the recital hoping for the chance to talk to you."

"So you aren't going to sell your house?" Her heart started an irregular thudding in her breast.

"Oh, I'm selling my house, all right," Kyle said. He smiled when her face fell, then added, "The one in California."

"You're not leaving," Mary said, unable to keep the joy out of her voice.

He shook his head. "It's like my neighbor says, once you've started clipping hedges, it's like clipping your own wings."

Mary raised a puzzled brow. "Meaning?"

"Meaning, I couldn't bear to see a nice big family house go to waste. Trouble is, I still need a family to go in it."

Mary turned into his arms then. "Oh, Kyle, I—"

"I'm sorry, Mary," Kyle interrupted. "I've said this all wrong again. But I guess what I mean is, I love you."

Her heart stopped. "Kyle, I—"

"Don't say it," he said, cutting her off once more. "All I want to know is whether you could have possibly changed your mind about marrying me."

Mary didn't give him the chance to break in again. "Ages ago!" she exclaimed. She wrapped her arms around his middle and squeezed tight.

Kyle held her close for a long, disbelieving moment before tilting her chin up with his forefinger to look into her face. "Ages ago?"

"Well, weeks, at least," Mary amended. "I thought I'd never get the chance to tell you. I love you, Kyle." Her heart felt as shiny and full as one of those bubbles Maggie was always blowing, and as delicate.

Their lips met briefly in a tentative yet achingly tender kiss. Then Kyle pulled away, shaking his head slowly, as if refusing to give credence to her words. "I realize what I did was terrible," he said, "thirteen years ago and then again last month. I know there's not a lot I can do to earn your trust."

"*I* was wrong, Kyle," Mary added. "What I wanted you to do thirteen years ago was unrealistic. You were just starting out."

"But you were only twenty yourself."

"Does it matter?" Mary asked. "It's been a long road for both of us. Long and confusing, sometimes."

"I can't believe it," Kyle said, half afraid this was only a dream. "There's so much I want to tell you, so many things we need to talk about."

"Such as?"

Kyle stared at her. She was wondrous, more beautiful to him now than she'd been thirteen years before. "Well, for starters, what would you say to a June wedding?"

"Hmm." Mary worried her brows dramatically. "That's possible, but of course, I might have to check my schedule."

Kyle laughed. "Think you could pencil me in?"

She leaned against him contentedly. "I think there's a definite chance that I'd even cancel a Thursday night at the Brass Kettle to attend my own wedding." Her eyes twinkled as she looked up at him. "Right now, the only important thing for me is that I love you, Kyle."

"Oh, Mary," Kyle said, renewing their hug with a weathered sigh. "I feel like I've waited thirteen years to hear you say that."

Mary laughed and snuggled happily against the fabric of his shirt. "I guess it just takes some of us longer than others." This time, when their lips joined, there was no tentativeness about it. The kiss was wholehearted, deep—like the love they bore for each other. And the waiting had made both all the more precious.

Mary's last words wafted through the windows of the house on the gentle evening breeze. Maggie lay on the couch, blowing a bubble and thinking how cool, how incredibly cool, life sometimes turned out to be. The jittery happy feeling inside her made her lose her creation, but as the bubble burst, she breathed in just in the nick of time.

* * * * *

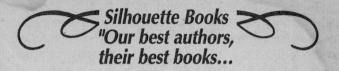

Silhouette Books
"Our best authors, their best books...

DIANA PALMER
Soldier of Fortune in February

ELIZABETH LOWELL
Dark Fire in February

LINDA LAEL MILLER
Ragged Rainbow in March

JOAN HOHL
California Copper in March

LINDA HOWARD
An Independent Wife in April

HEATHER GRAHAM POZZESSERE
Double Entendre in April

**When it comes to passion,
we wrote the book.**

BOBQ1

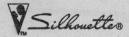

Take 4 bestselling love stories FREE

Plus get a FREE surprise gift!

Special Limited-time Offer

Mail to Silhouette Reader Service™

3010 Walden Avenue
P.O. Box 1867
Buffalo, N.Y. 14269-1867

YES! Please send me 4 free Silhouette Romance™ novels and my free surprise gift. Then send me 6 brand-new novels every month, which I will receive months before they appear in bookstores. Bill me at the low price of $2.19 each plus 25¢ delivery and applicable sales tax, if any.* That's the complete price and—compared to the cover prices of $2.75 each—quite a bargain! I understand that accepting the books and gift places me under no obligation ever to buy any books. I can always return a shipment and cancel at any time. Even if I never buy another book from Silhouette, the 4 free books and the surprise gift are mine to keep forever.

215 BPA ANRP

Name	(PLEASE PRINT)	
Address		Apt. No.
City	State	Zip

This offer is limited to one order per household and not valid to present Silhouette Romance™ subscribers. *Terms and prices are subject to change without notice. Sales tax applicable in N.Y.

HE'S MORE THAN A MAN, HE'S ONE OF OUR

CALEB'S SON
by Laurie Paige

Handsome widower Caleb Remmick had a business to run and a son to raise—alone. Finding help wasn't easy—especially when the only one offering was Eden Sommers. Years ago he'd asked for her hand, but Eden refused to live with his workaholic ways. Now his son, Josh, needed someone, and Eden was the only woman he'd ever trust—and the only woman he'd ever loved....

Look for *Caleb's Son* by Laurie Paige, available in March.

Fall in love with our **Fabulous Fathers!**

It's our 1000th
Silhouette Romance
and we're celebrating!

Join us for a special collection of love stories by the authors you've
loved for years, and new favorites you've just discovered.

It's a celebration just for you,
with wonderful books by
Diana Palmer, Suzanne Carey,
Tracy Sinclair, Marie Ferrarella,
Debbie Macomber, Laurie Paige,
Annette Broadrick, Elizabeth August
and MORE!

Silhouette Romance...vibrant, fun and emotionally rich! Take another
look at us!

As part of the celebration, readers can receive a FREE gift AND enter
our exciting sweepstakes to win a grand prize of $1000! Look for
more details in all March Silhouette series titles.

You'll fall in love all over again
with Silhouette Romance!

And now for
something completely different
from Silhouette....

SPELLBOUND
ROMANCE

Unique and innovative stories that take you into the world of paranormal happenings. Look for our special "Spellbound" flash—and get ready for a truly exciting reading experience!

In February, look for
One Unbelievable Man (SR #993)
by Pat Montana.

Was he man or myth? Cass Kohlmann's mysterious traveling companion, Michael O'Shea, had her all confused. He'd suddenly appeared, claiming she was his destiny—determined to win her heart. But could levelheaded Cass learn to believe in fairy tales...before her fantasy man disappeared forever?

Don't miss the charming, sexy and utterly mysterious
Michael O'Shea in
ONE UNBELIEVABLE MAN.
Watch for him in February—only from

Silhouette
ROMANCE™

SPELL2

**Fifty red-blooded, white-hot, true-blue hunks
from every State in the Union!**

Look for MEN MADE IN AMERICA! Written by some
of our most poplar authors, these stories feature fifty of
the strongest, sexiest men, each from a different state in
the union!

Two titles available every other month at your favorite
retail outlet.

In March, look for:

TANGLED LIES by Anne Stuart (Hawaii)
ROGUE'S VALLEY by Kathleen Creighton (Idaho)

In May, look for:

LOVE BY PROXY by Diana Palmer (Illinois)
POSSIBLES by Lass Small (Indiana)

You won't be able to resist MEN MADE IN AMERICA!

As seen on TV!
Free Gift Offer

With a Free Gift proof-of-purchase from any Silhouette® book,
you can receive a beautiful cubic zirconia pendant.

This gorgeous marquise-shaped stone is a genuine cubic
zirconia—accented by an 18" gold tone necklace.

(Approximate retail value $19.95)

Send for yours today...
compliments of ▼ *Silhouette*®

To receive your free gift, a cubic zirconia pendant, send us one original proof-of-
purchase, photocopies not accepted, from the back of any Silhouette Romance™,
Silhouette Desire®, Silhouette Special Edition®, Silhouette Intimate Moments® or
Silhouette Shadows™ title for January, February or March 1994 at your favorite retail
outlet, together with the Free Gift Certificate, plus a check or money order for $2.50
(do not send cash) to cover postage and handling, payable to Silhouette Free Gift Offer.
We will send you the specified gift. Allow 6 to 8 weeks for delivery. Offer good until
March 31st, 1994 or while quantities last. Offer valid in the U.S. and Canada only.

Free Gift Certificate

Name:_____

Address:_____

City: _____ State/Province: _____ Zip/Postal Code:_____

Mail this certificate, one proof-of-purchase and a check or money order for postage
and handling to: SILHOUETTE FREE GIFT OFFER 1994. In the U.S.: 3010 Walden
Avenue, P.O. Box 9057, Buffalo NY 14269-9057. In Canada: P.O. Box 622, Fort Erie,
Ontario L2Z 5X3

FREE GIFT OFFER   079-KBZ
ONE PROOF-OF-PURCHASE
To collect your fabulous FREE GIFT, a cubic zirconia pendant, you must include this
original proof-of-purchase for each gift with the properly completed Free Gift Certificate.

079-KBZ